WITHDRAWN

THE LONG NIGHT OF WINCHELL DEAR

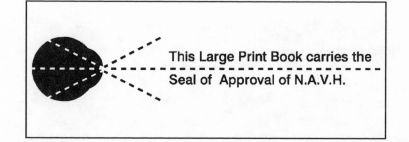

This Large Print Book carries the
Seal of Approval of N.A.V.H.

THE LONG NIGHT OF WINCHELL DEAR

A Novel

ROBERT JAMES WALLER

THORNDIKE PRESS

An imprint of Thomson Gale, a part of The Thomson Corporation

THOMSON

GALE

Detroit • New York • San Francisco • New Haven, Conn. • Waterville, Maine • London

THOMSON

GALE

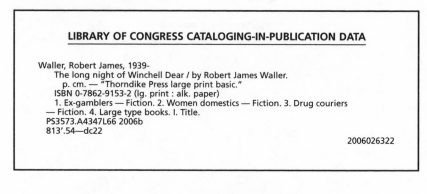

LIBRARY OF CONGRESS CATALOGING-IN-PUBLICATION DATA

Waller, Robert James, 1939-
   The long night of Winchell Dear / by Robert James Waller.
      p. cm. — "Thorndike Press large print basic."
   ISBN 0-7862-9153-2 (lg. print : alk. paper)
      1. Ex-gamblers — Fiction. 2. Women domestics — Fiction. 3. Drug couriers
   — Fiction. 4. Large type books. I. Title.
   PS3573.A4347L66 2006b
   813'.54—dc22

                                                                    2006026322

ISBN 13: 978-0-7862-9153-3

Published in 2006 in arrangement with Crown Publishers,
a division of Random House, Inc.

Printed in the United States of America on permanent paper.
10 9 8 7 6 5 4 3 2 1

To my wife, Linda,
who lived in and loved the high desert
for twenty years.

I am sorry I have not learned to play at cards. It is very useful in life: It generates kindness and consolidates society.

DR. SAMUEL JOHNSON

ONE

So, my nephew, listen to me and know my words: In the high desert, Time is an old, sly rider, a bandit of legend who will steal your days and take your woman and be smiling down at you as He boards the evening train.

And having remembered his uncle's words and having lived with the truth of them all the length of his fifty-one summers, Pablo Espinosa came hard and fast off the ridge of Guapa Mountain in full darkness. Seventy-two miles above the border and slipping on loose stones, clutching the green and swaying branches of piñon pines for balance, he began his descent toward Slater's Draw, where his silhouette would no longer pin him to the sky. Across the dry ground, his brown feet in the rope-and-rubber-tire sandals were taking him north as they had done before, in a relentless shuffle that regarded distance as nothing more than a vocation.

Above the sandals were floppy gray and thorn-ripped trousers, and above the trousers a shirt that might have been citron colored once but was faded now, with "Moorman's Lanes, Presidio, Texas" lettered on the back. Yesterday, a helicopter had spotted Pablo Espinosa as he worked his way around Santa Clara Peak, and afterward came the grinding roar of four-wheel-drive Broncos and radio talk he could hear imperfectly in the canyons below him while *la migra,* the Border Patrol, cut sign for his track. He'd hidden up through the daylight hours and now was trying to recoup his losses.

In a hurry and having reason to be, rolling a pebble over his tongue to bring up the last bit of moisture in his mouth, Pablo Espinosa was almost at his journey's end. The pack he carried weighed nearly a third as much as his 140 pounds, the miles and what the pack contained making it seem even heavier. He adjusted the straps, let himself down from a limestone outcropping, and headed toward the draw, the curl and cut of which would take him to quiet and good water, where the signal lamps of evening burned.

He hoped only two of the lamps would be lighted, for less or more meant he would have to wait in the darkness before going to the house and the completion of his work. The woman sometimes had visitors and did not want him coming by at those times. That had happened less than two weeks ago on his last run up here, and he was angry with her and said as much. But she had dismissed his annoyance with a wave of her hand and set tortillas and water before him.

Five hundred feet below and a third of a mile east of Pablo Espinosa lay the diamond-back. It of genus *Crotalus* and species *atrox,* on its belly and holding down its own special place in matters of form and function, was a month less than twenty years and an inch beyond seven feet. All day it had lain up under a mesquite tree, waking only twice when cattle grazed by. Now, with the sun well set and Del Norte peaks washed in the paleness of a three-quarter moon on its way to full, the air had cooled sufficiently for it to begin a night hunt.

Weighing sixteen pounds on its empty stomach, the diamondback came slowly out of its flat resting coil, and with the earth giving it purchase and converting horizontal curls into forward motion, it began to move across the high desert toward a ranch house. The route took it over short grass and past clumps of cholla cactus, through the loose dirt of a service road, winding, winding. On the other side of the road and fifty feet behind the rancher's house was a tank with a small leak forming a puddle from which the diamondback could suck its water.

Nearly across the road and sensing ground vibrations, the snake paused, came to alertness, eyes expressionless and always the same: black, fixed, unblinking. And the tongue flicking rapidly, conveying air particles to the Jacobson's organ in the roof of the mouth and thenceforth into the brain: smell. Its head came up, followed by part of the body and not quite into a full striking coil, holding there. But the vibrations receded, and after two minutes it slackened and continued on toward water, eventually crawling over boot prints put down only moments before.

So the high-desert night began to play itself like an old Victrola song. In the shadow of Guapa Mountain, a diamondback took water, a night bird called. A coyote howled, answered or joined seconds later, it was hard to tell which, by other coyotes. From the west, hard breathing and the nearly inaudible crunch of gravel beneath sandals as Pablo Espinosa picked his way along the bed of Slater's Draw. Coming off the ridge, he had noticed lights in the main ranch house far down to his right. He had seen them before on his other runs north and was not troubled, since he had been assured the old man who lived there was oblivious to what transpired in darkness.

A quarter mile northwest of the main house was another building, smaller and built of adobe and surrounded by scrub cedar, making it difficult to see from any distance how many lamps were lighted in the western windows. Pablo Espinosa would continue along the arroyo until he reached the big rock he had used before and would stand upon it and look over the edge of the draw, counting the window lamps. Please — his prayer went up to the Blessed Virgin — let there be two and only those. He could then relieve himself of the pack and drink good water, resting for a few hours before traveling south again to his home and family in Santa Helena. With luck, he would be picked up by *la migra* and given a ride to the crossing point near Castolon and would be home tomorrow evening. They would question him, of course, but he would say only that he had come to *el Norte* looking for work, and nothing could be proven otherwise. A sweet ride home on the American taxpayers' dollars, though Pablo Espinosa never thought of it quite that way. To him, the gringos' tolerant laws and innocent generosity simply made things easier.

Once more, a night bird. Once more, the coyotes. And almost finished with its drink, the diamondback again sensed movement, bringing its head out of the puddle and remaining still for five seconds before executing a slow backward crawl toward whatever cover it might find. Something had come to the other side of the water tank and was making sounds. Without a physiological apparatus of the kind normally associated with hearing, the snake perceived only some of those sounds, the ones causing even the faintest of vibrations in the substratum, such as human footsteps. In that way, *Crotalus atrox* could never be precisely sure of what surrounded it, could only react in a primitive fashion to the slice of reality baring itself to its receptors. For the diamondback, and as with most things counted among the living, existence when it was shorn of all that did not matter came down to food and danger and propagation of the species.

And the sounds were first the soft impact of old boots on the desert floor. Then beyond the snake's ability to hear, fingers swishing away debris from the tank's surface on which the moon rippled as the water moved and the slurping of a man drinking

14

from cupped hands.

The Indian finished his drink and slowly wiped the sleeve of a worn denim shirt across his mouth, glancing toward the kitchen windows of the ranch house fifty feet away. Lights from the kitchen spilled only a short way into the darkness, and through honeysuckle vines partially covering the window, the Indian could see an old man sitting at a table, handling cards.

At that moment, the Indian, long in the desert and attentive to the slightest shift in its cadence and feel, came aware of a presence close by and paused with the sleeve of his shirt partly across his mouth. He moved his eyes, nothing more, looking toward the other side of the tank, holding that position for nearly a minute. Then he smiled and placed his right forearm across his chest, palm of the hand downward, and moved it away from him with a slight waving motion in the old and understood language that had been the true sign of his ancestors 150 years before, when the People roamed the Comanchería and did as they chose. Long ago, when the People lived in freedom and with honor and the Comanche name was synonymous with fear and no quarter given or received.

He eased away from the tank, parted the

branches of a desert willow, and followed an oblique course away from the snake and toward Diablo Canyon six miles farther south. Looking up, he barely caught the moon-backed profile of someone descending a mountain ridge toward the jagged earth slash called Slater's Draw.

Hesitating, the Indian wondered if he should circle back to the small adobe where lights still burned. When he had left, the woman called Sonia was combing her black hair while she hummed and looked at herself in the bathroom mirror, her mouth tasting only a little acrid and her head only spinning slightly from the *sotol* she and the Indian had drunk. The mirror was cheap and caused a distortion. She supposed the rancher might buy her a new one if she asked, yet the bias was in the direction of making things narrower in whatever the mirror reflected, allowing the woman to feel younger than her age of fifty-four and slimmer than she truly was. And for that reason she said nothing and kept the mirror.

The Indian knew things were what they were and remained as such no matter how hard you might cry up for something different. In an unforgiving world, one trifled only with which one had to trifle by way of eating and drinking and getting along. And what

16

the woman did when he was not with her was nothing of his own. So thinking that and carrying a plastic sack with food she had given him, he moved on through the night toward his wood-and-canvas shelter in Diablo Canyon, stopping twice to look up at the moon and thank it for taking him home.

Whether the diamondback understood the moon or looked at it with gratitude is difficult to say. Maybe, maybe not. But the snake did seem to glance up now and then as it crawled toward what its acute sense of smell indicated might be a rabbit's nest with enough food to carry it for another few weeks. And it caused the stalks of yellow primrose to momentarily bend as it passed through them.

Two lights burned in windows a little east of Slater's Draw. Soft thump of a pack coming out of the draw and onto the ground above, lying there and containing what was worth slightly more than forty-five thousand dollars on the streets of America. Pablo Espinosa followed the pack, taking hold of a tree root with one hand and clawing earth with the other, pulling himself up and out.

He brushed arroyo dust off his clothes and caught his breath, looking around. Nothing. Quiet across the high desert, except for the shrill and distant scream of a mother rabbit too far away for Pablo Espinosa to hear.

Sitting in the kitchen of the main ranch house, Winchell Dear heard the scream. He'd heard it before and was neither surprised nor alarmed. Nature ran things with an iron fist in the desert: cries in the night, step over bones a month or two later. Death in the short grass.

Beneath the table, a dog older than Winchell Dear in equivalent dog years raised her head, sniffed, growled. The dog had come with the ranch, and there was a time when she would have been up and pushing open the screen door, on her way to investigate whatever was happening within the perimeter she defined as her place of duty and concern. But now, arthritic and tired from fourteen years of watchfulness, she merely laid her head on her paws and went back to sleep.

Winchell Dear said, "It's all right, girl. Let it go. Something got a rabbit, that's all."

He straightened his shoulders, shuffled cards, and glanced out at the night where vectors were closing toward him. He might have known that, or had a feeling about it, for old gamblers who have lived long and by their wits have a way of catching the smell of evil when it is still some distance off. Perhaps that was why he reached up and touched the little .380 Colt automatic slung in a holster under his left arm. Perhaps that was why he'd put on his good gray suit and custom-made boots and why he'd earlier made sure the ten-year-old Cadillac out in the garage was gassed and oiled. Something about this day just past and this night in progress did not feel right. Winchell Dear was at the ready, for reasons not altogether clear to him, something to do with faint vibrations in the substratum of his consciousness.

And the thought sideslipped into his mind, as it seemed to do now and then without any help from him, that if Jarriel hadn't taken off her clothes and danced naked on Cut Norway's pool table, he wouldn't have had sufficient cause to kick her butt down the ranch road and back to Las Vegas or wherever. And minus that, she might still be here with him and he wouldn't be so all alone. And she wouldn't be sending those nasty letters demanding money and making pestilential late night phone calls full of vague threats about what she was going to do if he didn't send something she called palimony, a word unfamiliar to both Winchell Dear and the laws of Texas.

He shuffled cards, looked out at the night, and began a nervous, faltering hum of the

song a Vegas musician had written about
him:

Sittin' at the table, with my best suit on,
blue suspenders tugging at my shoul-
ders . . .

A quarter mile northwest, in a small adobe
where two signal lamps of evening burned,
Sonia Dominguez combed her black hair
and looked in a mirror having the pleasant
flaw of making her seem younger than she
really was.

Two

Indian walking by moonlight. Diamond-back, with inexorable purpose or at least giving sign of purpose by its direction and movements, appearing to be only another shadow momentarily slung across the desert floor by whatever bent above it in the gusts of night wind, passing between and among those shadows until it was indistinguishable from the ground over which it traveled.

And Pablo Espinosa, pack up and centered, with only a quarter mile to go and legs getting on toward wobbly, letting fatigue have its way now that he was close to a place of resting. Next trip he'd buy a better flashlight for walking and demand a smaller load. He'd already decided that. Though one needed to be careful in making demands of the people with whom he dealt. At least he'd ask politely whether the weight could be reduced on his next run.

If not, he would sigh within himself and

carry what he was given and take the money. The pay for a single run north equaled six months of his younger sister's wages in the *maquiladoras,* American assembly plants splotched along the border. And for a poor man who used to be a campesino on forty acres of rocky ground, the dream of a small hacienda in the cool, wet mountains of the Sierra Madre had shifted from chimerical toward that which could be accomplished. That image, the dream of trees and water and grandchildren who would hold his hand and walk with him in the forest and fish clear streams, was what sustained him on those long nights and caused his feet to take him through the high and lonely desert mountains of *el Norte.*

In the adobe toward which Pablo Espinosa moved, Sonia Dominguez finished the hundred strokes through her hair and checked again to make sure two, and only two, lamps shone in the windows facing Slater's Draw. A mule, probably the little man with torn trousers and serious face — it was his turn, she reckoned — was due sometime tonight. He would be hungry and would smell bad. She would give him tortillas and make him sleep on the floor, then see to it he was gone well before sunrise. And she would wash the floor afterward and air all three rooms of the adobe.

Up at the main house, Winchell Dear looked at the Regulator clock above the sink, which now read 11:43, and that time being only seven minutes further on from when he'd last checked it. He simultaneously shuffled two decks of playing cards as he began his evening's second game of Virginia reel solitaire, a game challenging enough to be of interest to a master poker player.

Big west and small north from Winchell Dear's kitchen lay El Paso, sprawled and still mostly awake under a three-quarter moon. There on the hard and grease-stained surface of a truck stop, a man the same height and not two pounds heavier than Pablo Espinosa stared at the moon through mercury vapor lights. He moved out of the glare and looked up again at more stars than he could ever remember seeing through the haze of Los Angeles. The Milky Way had never been this clear to him, running as it did in a soft, wide streak across the night.

"Marty, you ready, or you just going to look at the sky for the rest of your life?"

"No."

"No what?"

"I'm ready. You ready?"

While his partner stuffed change in a wallet, Marty walked to the front of a cream-colored Lincoln Continental and squatted. Being careful not to soil his expensive suit and the eighty-dollar white shirt beneath it, he reached under the passenger-side fender and touched the metal boxes duct-taped to engine supports.

"Everything okay under there?"

"Yeah, okay. The boxes are still tight."

The Connie wheeled out of the truck stop and nosed onto I-10, accelerating by the force of a Cole Haan loafer special-ordered in width EE and length thirteen.

"Check the map again," the driver said. "This goddamn country doesn't make any sense, goes on forever. Feel like I'm in a dumb-fuck desert or on some foreign planet or something."

Marty flipped on the overhead light and unfolded a Texas map, running his finger along the roads ahead of them. "I'd say we're about three hours, or a little more, west of that town called Clear Signal. We stay on I-10 till Van Horn, then cut south and east on 90."

He fished a piece of paper from his inside jacket pocket. "This handwritten map we were given shows the place we're looking for is another fifteen miles past the town, near something called Slater's Draw. Supposed to

24

be a bridge and a sign saying that, 'Slater's Draw.' It's almost twelve now. We should be there about three. That'll work out about right, everybody being asleep and all. Shouldn't it?"

"Marty, turn off the light. It shines in my eyes, can't see good when it's on."

"Just a second. I'm looking for the location of that border patrol station. I marked it earlier . . . yeah, here it is. It's on I-10, about an hour up the road from us, near Sierra Blanca. Sierra Blanca, that'd mean 'White Mountain' or something like that in English, wouldn't it?"

"Marty, would you *please* goddamn turn off the goddamn light?"

Marty folded the highway map, tucked away the handwritten map, and flipped off the light. "Once we clear that border patrol station, I'll feel better. Think they'll shake us down?"

"Nah, they won't bother us. They'll be looking for wetbacks. That's what I was told."

"I hope you're right. I don't like being without the hardware. Getting under the car and undoing duct tape ain't exactly what you'd call a fast pull."

Marty twisted his neck and looked out the passenger-side window, trying to see the sky

25

again and wishing he'd studied the moon more than he had during a messy life, which in a way Marty couldn't grasp seemed to be disappearing while he lived it. He'd been thinking recently about taking up a religion, something that would provide focus to his time among the living. Maybe the Church of the Latter-day Saints or Jehovah's Witnesses. Representatives from both sects had knocked on his apartment door in the last month and talked with him. He'd studied the pamphlets they'd left, but it all seemed pretty confusing and involved certain commitments and pledges he wasn't sure he could fold into his work and lifestyle.

"Dumb idea anyway, taping the guns up under there," he said, sliding lower until his knees were bent and his rear was on the edge of the seat. "Think that'd fool the Border Patrol if they got serious about us? Shit, no. Dumb idea, right?"

"Well, that's what we were told to do. Just following orders." The driver looked over and down at Marty. "Hey, what'n hell you up to, working on your limbo dance or something?"

"I'm looking for the goddamn moon. What you think I'd be doing way down here? Dumb idea, that's what, taping the guns up under the fender. Christ, I see it now. What

26

a moon out there! See it?"

Marty possessed an irritating habit of ending almost any topic he happened to be on with a question, sometimes requiring an answer, sometimes not. And it could drive you crazy, because if you were around him, you spent half your time deciding whether or not an answer was necessary and, if it seemed that way, the other half thinking one up.

Aside from that, he was a little nutty but generally useful, and the best part of him was his absolute lack of conscience together with being a good weapons man. Marty lacked a certain amount of overpowering intelligence, yet he was cool when the work was in progress and never looked back and always seemed to be hungry after a job. He said killing was like sex in that respect. But he never ate until the guns were cleaned and loaded again. Had a rule about that and stuck to it.

The driver thought about Marty's complexities, then shook his head and lit a Marlboro, accelerating a little more, pushing the Connie hard into the West Texas night.

THREE

Everyone in Clear Signal, Texas, including the morning coffee group down at the Ocotillo Cafe, was pretty sure Winchell Dear didn't get those seventy sections east of town by doing smart cattle business. That conclusion followed from the evidence before them: Winchell Dear leased out the grazing rights after acquiring the land, and if he'd been a real rancher, he would never have done that. Of course, he'd slapped his brand on thirty head of longhorns he kept mostly as walking scenery, but pets didn't count. Plus, according to Jack Stark, who held the grazing lease, Winchell Dear was letting an Indian squat on his land.

So they'd figured out that much and wondered why the old Circle F had ever gone over to this stranger from somewhere else in the first place. Somebody did point out, however, that somebody else remembered there had been a border patrolman named

Dear stationed around Clear Signal a long time ago, and maybe this Winchell fellow was related to him in some way.

Said one, while they were getting ready to leave the Ocotillo and matching coins to determine who would pay for the coffee: "You know, the Cobblers owned that Circle F from almost the beginnings of West Texas. Old Fayette Cobbler used to say he'd come out here in aught five with nothing more than a horse, a saddle, and a hard-on and would probably leave with nothing more than his saddle. But he killed more'n one rustler, cleared the lions from Guapa Mountain, and worked his ass off, building that place from the ground up . . . him and his wife and wetback labor. Never was a real big ranch, but forty-five thousand acres ain't all that shabby as a way of leaving something behind. They took a little silver out of Guapa Mountain, and that helped him get by some of the thin years."

Said another: "Well, things have a way of deteriorating by the third generation. Young Rick Cobbler always seemed a lot more interested in going skiing up at Ruidoso and hanging around Las Vegas than he did in ranching."

Said a third: "Something tells me Las Vegas had a lot to do with Rick giving up the

29

Circle F and leaving town. He used to drop quite a bit right here when the nonstop poker game over at the Leland Hotel was still running. Was known as a loose player. Some folks ran into him a while back up in Vegas, at the Desert Inn, I think they said it was. Said he was drinking awful heavy, all roostered up and raving on about card cheats and that, by God, the cheats weren't getting away with any more cheating if he had anything to say about it, and, by God, in addition he was going to fix somebody's wagon. Rick always was hotheaded, you know. By the way, notice what that Winchell Dear renamed the place?"

Said the first: "Damn, you might be right, Jake. I never put all that together. Hell, yes, calls it the Two Pair. That makes some kind of sense, don't it?" He sketched Winchell Dear's brand in the air while he talked.

"And talking about pairs, did that woman he brought out here with him ever have a set!" Jake rolled his eyes upward and let out a short whistle of appreciation for the content of images still recalled. "What the hell was her name ... Jemima, Janene, Jarrel, something like that? How old you figure she was, forty maybe? She sure as hell had the Clear Signal T-shirt-and-tight-jeans prize well in hand all the time she was here."

The others nodded, conjuring up their memories of Jarriel Piper pushing a grocery cart up and down the aisles of the Food Basket. Seemed she was always followed or met by a line of cowhands pushing carts and grinning back and forth at one another like schoolboys exchanging dirty pictures.

Said the third, "Yeah, heard one time she was Miss Montana in a beauty contest. When she was younger, of course."

Said the fourth, "Well, getting back down to earth, in a manner of speaking, two pair ain't much of a poker hand, and that land's about the same caliber. Deep-well place. Need to drill twelve to fifteen-hundred feet before you find anything. Ol' Fayette used to say about his water out there, 'If I don't get it from heaven, got to pull it up from hell.' "

Everybody laughed as they stood up, ready to leave.

"Goddamn, miss old Fayette since the lung cancer, I guess it was, got him eighteen, twenty years ago. Let's see, wasn't it about ten years after Fayette passed on that Fayette junior died when that snorty son-of-a-bitching gelding of his went over on him in Diablo Canyon?"

One and two nodded.

"That was one oily bronc. Fayette junior used to say that hisself. Said if he didn't know better, he'd've sworn they'd never cut the horse. Gelding came back over on him and saddle horn broke his breastbone and four ribs. Wasn't enough chest structure left to help him breathe. Six hours passed before Rick found him dead and the horse grazing off to one side, just quietly towing along Fayette junior, whose boot was all tangled up in a stirrup."

The shadows outside the café were sharp and clean in the desert sun as they said good-bye, and each pulled his hat low and went his own way on the morning of the day that would bring the long night of Winchell Dear.

FOUR

Under kitchen lights reflecting off walls of dark wood and partially absorbed and mellowed almost to amber by that effect, Winchell Dear finished his third game of solitaire and began shuffling the cards again. The Regulator clock above the sink read 12:40. The overhead fan turned slowly, squeaking on every fourth revolution.

And the hands of Winchell Dear: fingers long, running slim to bony. The hands, liver-spotted but still light and feathery and like a magician's, doing the old classic shuffle his father had taught him. Half the cards from the top of the pack with his right hand, other half in the left, put both halves end to end. Thumbs on the side of the cards toward him, forefingers on the cards with knuckles bent, other three fingers supporting the cards opposite the thumbs. Riffle the halves together with the thumbs, loosen grip, slide them into a single block. Cut, pull out the bottom half, lay it on the top half. Do it again, then once more and once more after that.

Winchell Dear could execute a four-shuffle in slightly more than fifteen seconds, including the cuts, and never looked as if he were hurrying while he was doing it. He'd had a lot of practice. And while he riffled the cards, he thought of Lucinda Miller and hoped she was doing well. Lucinda was a hell of a lot better woman than Jarriel, and on nights like this, especially on nights like this one, he mourned the passing of what they'd had at one time. Quiet snap of cards and Winchell Dear thinking he ought to give Lucinda a call and check on her general well-being.

Fifty-two years back along the curls and wobbles of a chancy life and on the occasion of Winchell Dear's fifteenth birthday in 1938, his father took him into the desert. They sat in a Ford coupé and looked across the Rio Grande toward the Carmens rising high and rocky in northern Mexico, dirt and sand riding hard on a late afternoon wind and pinging against the car's metal parts. Little cyclones of dust spurted up and twirled across the ground in front of them, flamenco quick and dying even as they formed and danced.

After lighting a cigar and puffing on it for something near a minute, his father pointed the cigar toward Mexico. "Mexicans are basically good people. Like 'em. They've got a screwed-up country, but I like the people."

He smoked for another minute, then spoke quietly. "Winchell, the reason I brought you out here is to talk a little about your future, so I'll get right to it. To my way of thinking, there's only three things a man needs to know about as a way of getting on with his life, and they all start with *p:* pistols, poker, and fast Pullman trains. Those'll protect you, sustain you, and get you where you need to go."

His father reached behind the front seats and pulled out a .44-caliber revolver, an 1887 Remington that had been hard used by the look of it, and three boxes of bullets along with two decks of playing cards still in their wrappers. "The cards are new, the pistol belonged to a friend of mine, Leo Dawkins . . . you've heard me mention him a time or two, I think."

Winchell thought he'd heard the name before, but it seemed as if his father knew everybody scattered along the 1,300 miles of river separating Texas and Mexico, and Sam Dear was always telling one story or another, the pieces of which kind of ran together and lost their separate identities after a while. Winchell probably had heard about Leo Dawkins somewhere in all of that, and as he thought on it, he was pretty sure he remembered something about an abortive cavalry charge.

Sure enough. His father waved the cigar in a direction that could be described as generally west and said, "Leo was the only one killed when the Seventh Cavalry made its famous assault against Pancho Villa near Juarez. Last true and great cavalry charge in American history, led by Colonel Tommy 'Pink Whiskers' Tompkins no less. They tell me it was really something, starting out as a thing of beauty and grandeur, before it degenerated into chaos. Leo's horse went into an irrigation ditch at full scoot, broke his neck — Leo's, that is. Don't know how the horse came out of it. Leo was a good man to make horse tracks with, and I can tell you that's not the way he would've picked to die if he'd been given any choice in the matter. Anyway, his gun came over to me through his sister, and I'm giving it to you. It's a little more iron than you're ready for right now, but you'll grow into it."

Winchell turned the heavy pistol over in his hands and noticed how the late desert sun reflected off the barrel, while his father smoked and looked toward Mexico.

After a time, the man who loved the river and thought well of the Mexican people, and carried his badge and revolver everywhere he went, talked some more. "Winchell, don't tell your mother about all this. She'd have a fit. She won't mind about the gun; that's just part of a man's ordinary tool kit out here. But the cards are something altogether different.

"Your mother keeps thinking you ought to be a doctor or lawyer or such. She's never understood men all that well, sees things from a woman's perspective, which I suppose is natural, and what I'm trying to get across is the notion of independence. I've worked for the government most of my life, and I'm here to tell you that's not the way to go. And doctors and lawyers are just retail merchants, in most ways, dependent on people walking up to them for their services.

"Now" — his father became expansive, his language broadening and his gestures growing until they swept across the border and back again, along the big river and over all the spaces where latitude and leeway might be found — "learn to play poker and learn it better than anyone else . . . *there's* a way to earn your living. Free as that Harris' hawk circling over there and beholden to no one. Got that?"

Winchell nodded, a little confused and never having given one single thought to playing cards for a living and not at all sure that was how he wanted his life to turn. He'd been leaning toward becoming a cowboy or a border patrolman like his father. Maybe even a mining engineer, like the men in high lace-up boots and broad-brimmed hats he'd seen over at the Terlingua cinnabar diggings. He didn't know for sure what mining engineers did, but he admired their clothes and the way they walked around with papers in their hands, giving directions to those who did the dirty jobs. Being a mining engineer had its appeal, outdoor work and giving orders. Hard to beat that combination.

Sam Dear went on, "I'm not a real expert, but I know a few things, and I'm going to start by showing you how to shuffle cards. After that, I'll teach you the basics of the various poker games. But the mark of a professional is being able to handle the cards in a light and easy way, make 'em dance and talk, make 'em go where you want 'em to go and do what you want 'em to do.

"When you get halfway decent with the basics, I'll introduce you to Fain Bracquet . . . you've seen him, the slick-looking fellow who hangs out at the Thunder Butte Store. They don't call him a chaparral fox for nothing. Fain's one of the great card cheats in the Southwest, and he can show you what to watch for in that line of bad doings. You'll notice he always dresses up like a sore toe and never seems to work for a living. That's because Fain Bracquet knows things other people don't. When he's through teaching you the tricks, you'll be able to spot most card cheats and hustlers right off. Get good enough and you won't need to cheat, and you shouldn't ever do that anyway. Like I said, all I want you to learn from Fain is what to watch out for.

"Got to make do for yourself out there, Winchell. It's called capitalism, I guess, and this so-called Great Depression ain't showing much sign of ending. Always people gambling, however, hard times or not. That seems kind of odd, but it's true. Something to do with faith in investing a little money to try to make a lot of money in spite of all the odds against them, usually losing their little money on the dreams of big money when they could've been investing their little money in something better and slowly working up to big money."

Young Winchell was pretty clouded up by what his father was saying. It all sounded like a risky and somewhat scary adult world of cheaters and cardsharps and tough men who probably wouldn't tolerate excuses or inexperience. Sounded like a pretty uncertain way of making a living compared with being a cowboy or border patrolman or mining engineer.

"Well, Winchell, what do you think about all this?"

At fifteen, the boy was still a little gawky in the movements of both his mind and his body. He gave his father a half-shy grin and shrugged, not knowing what to say for sure and staying quiet.

"Well, you can give it a try, and if it doesn't work out, that's okay, too. Winchell, I'm not saying you *got* to do the things I've been talking about. Just offering some different choices from those you might be considering."

They drove back toward home, Sam Dear holding the wheel with both hands, cold cigar clenched in the left side of his mouth. The coupé bounced over rocks and cactus while Winchell held the big pistol in his lap and studied it.

"It's a gate-loading gun, Winchell." His father was talking past the cigar, wiggling it up and down with almost every word. "Doesn't flip open like my service revolver. Move that little doojiggy back of the cylinder, and you'll be able to see one chamber at a time. Ejector rod under the barrel pulls back, kicks out the empty shell, and you're ready to stick a new one in the chamber. Single-action, too, so you got to cock the hammer before it'll fire. It's a little slow on the reload but still one of the best old-time pistols ever made. We'll go out behind the house tomorrow, and I'll show you how the whole thing works."

Winchell Dear moved the doojiggy and looked into the hollow space of an empty .44-caliber chamber. It was a big space, and his little finger fit partway into the opening.

Just before they reached the four-room house roughed together out of adobe and serving as both a home and a border patrol station, his father spoke again. "Winchell, never drink while you're gambling, shifts your risk propensity. And never gamble on the blood sports, on a dog or cockfight, or on a contest between a bull and a bear. Those are not honorable.

"And horse racing, while more noble, still lacks the element of personal control over the outcomes. Same goes for roulette, keno, and the rest of those pure-chance games. Life's enough of a gamble all by itself without intentionally putting yourself in situations you can't control. That's something I learned too late, and why I feel kind of stuck where I am."

There it was again. Winchell had heard it all before, from his father, from other men. Not the exact words so much, but rather the sound and feel of the words, the unspoken thoughts behind them. His father, other men, a sense of things beyond their reach, giving off the impression of dreams they'd never got around to living out. But then, it was a time of limits, when things were not going the way everyone thought they would go on forever back in the twenties.

As they came into the yard, if dirt and sand and cactus passed for a yard, Winchell's mother was taking down wash from the lines, fighting a late afternoon wind driving grit into the clean laundry. The life of a border patrolman could be hard and lonely, when he might be riding the river for days at a time. But Winchell Dear always thought his mother's life was even harder and lonelier in ways he couldn't quite define. Her face, dried and darkened from wind and sun, made her look older than her thirty-eight years, but then all the women who lived in the high desert looked that way. So did the men, of course, but somehow it looked more natural on them, to Winchell's way of thinking.

Nancy Dear smiled readily and laughed at times, yet Winchell would catch her staring up at the stars at night or looking long and far out a window toward the north in the quiet of early mornings. She'd come from a big ranching family, the Winchells up near Odessa, and had been accustomed to the bustle and chatter of people coming and going. Hardly anyone ever dropped by their border patrol station, unless it was a Texas Ranger or another patrolman to pick up Winchell's father and go off with him somewhere in pursuit of smugglers or rustlers or whatever.

Once every two or three months, the family would travel up to Clear Signal for supplies. While his father met with various lawmen and stocked up on ammunition and bridles and rope at Big Bend Hardware and General Merchandise, Nancy Dear spent hours looking over cloth and buttons in the dry goods store on Front Street. She always seemed especially quiet and lonely on their way back down to the border, not saying much while the coupé rocked and slithered along the dirt road. She just stared through the side window and fretted with the collar of her dress, looking out and up and along the arch of what might have been, while at the same time not altogether dissatisfied with what had come to be.

Young Winchell Dear was lonely, too, though the fact that he'd been lonely back then never occurred to him until later on in his life. It was simply the way things were and the way things went, and it wouldn't have done any good to complain about them even if he'd thought about complaining.

His mother homeschooled him for three hours after breakfast and for another hour after lunch. The rest of each day was his. He fished the Rio Grande, hunted deer and javelina with the family's .30-30 saddle gun, brought down blue quail and ducks with the shotgun, and collected Indian artifacts. Sometimes he took one of the horses and went off to explore Indian ruins or, in cooler weather, simply watched the shift and blow of clouds streaming down like a river over the top of the Carmens and then hitting the warmer temperatures below and lifting again to hide all sight of the mountains.

Or he'd walk out of view of the house, sit down at a flat rock, and practice shuffling cards, all the while wondering at how curious it was, the attraction of humans to the desultory lurch and caprice of cardboard slices with numbers and pictures on them.

And, even more curious, that you could actually earn a living by mastering the cards and learning to make chance move in your direction more often than not. Every week or so, his father would drive the two of them someplace away from the house and show him the basic poker games and how the hands ranked, dealing cards on the car seats.

On a Saturday six months after Winchell Dear received the pistol and cards, his father took him out in the desert, telling Winchell to bring along a deck of cards but not to let his mother see him doing it. "We'll take the forty-four, make it look like we're going to do a little shooting."

They went out to Winchell's flat rock, and his father smiled. "Show me how you handle the cards, Winchell."

The boy did as he was told, shuffling, dealing, cutting, and looked up at his father.

"Pretty good, I'd say. Pretty *darn* good, in fact. Little more practice is needed on your shuffle, but good enough for right now. Saw Fain Bracquet at the Thunder Butte Store yesterday and told him what I had in mind about him teaching you a few things. Said he'd be glad to do just that. By the way, what's better, a straight or three of a kind?"

Winchell Dear didn't pause. "Straight."

"Two pair or three of a kind?"

"Three of a kind."

"Two pair and jacks up, or one pair and aces up?"

"Always two pair over one pair."

"Two pair or high pair?"

"Two pair."

"Flush or a straight?"

"Flush."

"What're the odds of hitting a royal flush on the opening deal in straight poker?"

"Six hundred fifty thousand to one."

"Good. Might see one or two royal flushes in a lifetime, so don't count on the big-kill hands. Most of the money over the long haul is made by smart play of ordinary hands. Work things up a bit at a time, keep piling today's gains on top of yesterday's, which is kind of a general rule for life, what I call the value of the small increment.

"Now, what's the chance of converting two pairs into a full house with a one-card draw?"

Winchell always struggled remembering those particular odds and hesitated. He looked up at his father and said, "About . . . eleven to one?"

"That's right, but you've got to get real smooth with the calculations, so smooth you can concentrate on the flow of the game and not the numbers. You're coming along. Keep at it."

His father smiled again. "Your mother said your math lessons have been picking up lately and that she couldn't figure out why. Let's head on over to the store and look up Fain Bracquet. I don't cotton to his ethics, but I do respect his skill.

"And let me warn you about Fain. He can talk your right arm off and whisper in the hole. Has a tendency to think he's something of an expert on everything, including women, horses, and water witching. Concentrate on what he says about card playing and ignore all the rest of the corral dust he hands out."

In the autumn of 1938, the temperature was still running over a hundred degrees by midday, though you could tell by the look of things that it would be cooling down a bit in another week or two. Something about how the late afternoon shadows latticed out from the chollas and Thompson yuccas. Something about how the wind felt as it switched around to the north and caused the Texas flag hanging from a pole on the Thunder Butte Store to flutter and occasionally snap with a sharp *whuk*.

When they arrived at the store, Fain Bracquet was sitting on the front porch, tilted back in a chair with boots on the railing. He was intently studying a gold watch affixed to a gold chain, as if his world were coming to an end and he was trying to figure out just how much time he might have left.

FIVE

In the mind of Winchell Dear, it all felt like a story sometimes, his life when he thought back on it, as if it had never happened yet was being told. Life as a campfire version of someone else's existence. A devious falsehood of pieces strung together as one fire rose in a prairie night and a second, the same fire but dying now, turned to warm ashes while long riders pulled their blankets around them and slept after the telling.

Winchell Dear shuffled and dealt and arrayed the cards before him, but not feeling like another hand of Virginia reel solitaire, he stood and ran a glass of water. He leaned against the sink, sipped from the glass, and then emptied it in the drain. From a cupboard above the sink, he took a bottle of Old Charter. Tipped the bottle, studied it — a third full. He poured two fingers' worth and carried the glass with him into the billiards room. It was coming up on one o'clock in the morning.

A quarter mile northwest, dehydrated and exhausted, came Pablo Espinosa through the darkness, his relentless shuffle evolving into something more like a blind stagger by the time he reached the adobe. Even in the cool desert night he was sweating through his shirt for about the hundredth time on this run and knew he smelled worse than a five-day-old lion kill in midsummer. He rapped lightly on one of the west windows. The woman appeared and slid open the window, holding out her hands and saying nothing. He gave her the pack and followed it in, climbing over the sill.

Immediately, she began haranguing him about how bad he smelled, telling him to get out of her bedroom and into the kitchen. Pablo noticed the bedroom didn't smell all that good, either, drenched with the heavy and commingled scents of sex and *sotol* and sweat generated from something other than honest labor. The bed was unmade and rumpled, with an empty bottle lying on one of the pillows. On the table beside the bed was the stub of a candle, with cold drippings surrounding it like a skirt and flowing from the candleholder onto the table itself.

While the woman named Sonia heated frijoles and rice and goat meat of the form called *cabrito*, Pablo Espinosa sat at her green-painted table. The table had drop-down leaves and was scored deeply in several places, the scars and stains coming from years of steady use by the Cobblers and later by those who worked for them. He drank three glasses of water and then sat quietly with his head in his hands, not being able to recall ever having been so tired. The run north required a young man's legs and a young man's spirit. Pablo Espinosa owned neither and knew his days of packing for the cartel would soon come to an end. But not before a piece of land in the high, cool, and watered Sierra Madre was his, so he hoped. And in spite of his fatigue, Pablo Espinosa once again forced bleary hope into a con-tract with himself as he sat at the woman's table, reinforcing the covenant with visions of green trees and running water.

By the time his food was ready, he'd folded his arms on the table, put his head on the fold, and was sleeping.

The woman shook him harshly, saying, "Wake up, old man. Eat your food, *then* sleep for a few hours and be gone from here."

Groggy, Pablo Espinosa slowly wrapped the frijoles and rice and *cabrito* into a tortilla and began to eat, looking down at his plate and not at the woman. She leaned against the stove and watched him, thinking she ought to report how fatigued this one called Pablo Espinosa was each time he arrived and perhaps suggest he be replaced with some-one more able. There was much law in this area — Texas Rangers, the Border Patrol, DEA people, state troopers, and other po-lice. They knew the Pablo Espinosas were running through the days and nights toward places in *el Norte,* and Sonia Dominguez did not want this old man to be caught and talk-ing freely about his drop point.

He glanced up at her, eyes watery and hands shaking from fatigue. Mother Maria, Sonia Dominguez thought, it looked as if he might go to sleep with a tortilla in his hand and be sitting there like some statue carved as a tribute to the peasant life.

"I have placed a blanket on the floor beside you. I will wake you two hours before dawn." She pinched her nose. "Do you smell this bad when you climb on your wife? She must be a forgiving woman if you do."

"I think I have a fever," Pablo Espinosa said.

"You need sleep, old man, that's all."

So saying, she carried the pack into her bedroom and closed the door behind her. Later she would redistribute the load into a

52

suitcase, after skimming two ounces for her own stash in Long Rifle Cave. The young musician who dealt the skim in Clear Signal always told her what good *mota* it was when he paid her for a new batch, at a rate of one hundred and fifty dollars for each quarter pound and for which he would collect four hundred dollars by parceling it down even further and selling it to his friends, who smoked it and escaped for a while from lives going nowhere or giving every appearance of leading in that direction. After a while, though, the comfort became the cause, its magic obscuring that shift even as it happened.

In three nights, Sonia Dominguez would pack two suitcases in a wheelbarrow and take them to a hiding place under the highway bridge running over Slater's Draw. The man called Norpie would come at two A.M. in his new Buick, timing his approach so his would be the only car on that desolate stretch of West Texas highway. He would stop on the bridge, honk quickly four times as a signal, and take the suitcases. He would leave her two empty ones in their place, pay her, and the cycle would begin again. In a few more years, even though she sent a third of the money back to Mexico for her mother and sister, Sonia Dominguez would have enough saved to buy a house in the nicer part of Clear Signal and be able to live into a decent, quiet old age.

Through her bedroom door, she could hear Pablo Espinosa snoring and shook her head in disgust. He even held to the old-fashioned sandals instead of the lug-soled hiking boots or sneakers worn by the others. None of the coyotes demonstrated any *estilo*, any style, including the Anglos who came through occasionally. Well, except for the young one named Franklin. He'd been a professional surfer at one time, so he said, though Sonia Dominguez wasn't quite sure what that involved. He'd seemed to show interest in her on his last run and perhaps thought some possibilities existed out in the future, only after he had bathed and eaten, of course. But that would not come about, the mixing of business and pleasure. Sonia Dominguez had her own rules and stuck to them.

After winding her bedside clock and setting the alarm, Sonia Dominguez took off her cotton robe and lay down on rumpled sheets, naked and fanning herself with a magazine. The alarm was set for well before dawn, but the loutish hombre called Espinosa would be sleepy, and it would take a good rousting to make him get up and leave her wallpapered kitchen on time.

She raised and parted the curtains on a south-facing window. The old man, Winchell Dear, apparently was still awake, since there were lights on in the main house. But she had learned his ways and knew him to be a night person. Tomorrow she would cook his food and clean his rooms and make his bed, in the way she had done for the last two years, being careful not to disturb the mean-looking little *pistola* hanging from the right-hand post of his headboard.

He was a strange, quiet man of few words, often handling cards, the sound of them riffling behind her sometimes while she worked. She watched him secretly and marveled at the light, easy touch he had with the cards. And she wondered about the *pistola,* if he really knew how to use it or only kept it near him for assurance, like a baby with its blanket or a traditional Mexican woman with her home.

A year had passed since he had thrown out the loud and demanding *gringita* — and what a fight that had been, the woman screaming obscenities and saying he'd known how she was when he'd brought her out here.

But, all of it considered, looked at six ways and accounted for, Sonia Dominguez had a pretty good deal and knew it. Unlike that wild Rick Cobbler before him, Winchell Dear was unfailingly polite, lenient in what he asked of her, and often gone for a week or two — sometimes a month — in that dark blue Cadillac of his, which made her night work even easier. She thought of all those things as she drifted into sleep just after midnight. The Comanche's scent remained on her pillow, and she smiled, thinking about him and how lean and hard he felt.

But she smiled even more when she started thinking about the house she would someday buy in the nicer part of Clear Signal, Texas. Not bad for a woman who had groveled and feared deportation for years, until the 1986 amnesty allowed her to become an American citizen. Not bad at all and some better than that.

SIX

Slightly more than ninety minutes southeast of El Paso, the cream-colored Lincoln Continental rolled easy through the little town of Corvalla, Texas.

Marty pointed. "Look over there. Sign says, 'Electrical Supplies and Fresh Ostrich Meat.' What the hell kind of business combination is that? Hey, there's a convenience store still open. Really think we need gas already?"

"Can't be too careful out here, Marty. It's about a million miles between gas stations. Notice, we haven't been able to get even shit-kickin' music on the radio for the last forty miles. Nothing, just static."

"That's true," Marty said. "What kind of place don't even get one radio station at night?"

"This place," the driver sighed, as he pulled alongside the pumps at the Amigos store.

"We should've flown to El Paso and rented a car. Why didn't we do that?"

The driver was opening his door. "Marty, checking as airline baggage what we got in those metal boxes taped to the engine struts would have been a little risky. Might have gotten lost."

"Yeah, you're right." Marty was opening the passenger-side door. "I forgot about that. Didn't have any problems at the border patrol checkpoint at Sierra Blanca, though, did we? Waved us right on through like you said. Glad I'm a white man, ain't you?"

The driver, whose mother was Mexican and birthed him at fifteen, inserted the nozzle in the Connie's tank, looked up at the Texas night, and didn't answer. He'd never known his mother. She'd crossed the border early in her fifteenth year and delivered, in that way making sure her child would be an American citizen. Afterward, she'd been sent back to Mexico for reasons never explained and left him to be raised by a distant aunt and uncle. He'd heard it said that his Anglo father was of fair complexion and worked the fishing boats out of San Diego.

Marty walked to the front of the car and stretched his arms over his head, rising on his toes and bouncing slightly. "My back's bothering me a little, all this riding. Back

58

problems run in my family. Your back ever bother you on long drives?"

"Marty, go in there and see if they got any decent coffee." Ignoring Marty's question, the driver squeezed the gasoline fill-lever harder, as if it would hurry things along, even though the pump was running at maximum speed. "Get us a couple of big cups if they do. I'll take mine black with a little sugar."

The driver wondered what the minimum IQ was for being able to clean and load a Beretta 93R machine pistol. Firing one didn't require any brains, that was for sure, or Marty would have been out of work a long time ago.

Inside the Amigos store, Marty was complaining about the lack of fresh-brewed coffee. The teenage girl tending things chewed gum and leaned against the cigarette rack, staring at him, fingers on her right hand fiddling with three rings on the left.

"Don't you ever think some late night travelers might be needing a good cup of coffee?"

"We're about at closing time," said the girl. "Never make fresh coffee after eleven o'-clock. That's the owner's rule. Too much waste, he says."

"Well, that don't make any sense, does it?"

Marty was irritated by the coffee situation and almost as put out by the girl's drawly way of speaking. Something about how the words sounded as they came out of her mouth bothered him. He wasn't sure why, just bothered him, that's all. The driver had said this whole region was about as far gone as a dumb-fuck desert, and Marty was starting to agree with that point of view.

When the driver came in and pulled out his wallet, the girl stepped over and looked at a digital readout. "That'll be seven ninety," she said.

"They don't have no goddamn fresh coffee." Marty's voice showed clear and present irritation.

"We don't make fresh coffee after eleven," the girl said, repeating the owner's rule and handing a dime in change to the driver. "We're closin' in fifteen minutes."

"Don't make any goddamn sense, that's what." Marty was studying key chains with steer heads on them.

"Doesn't have to make sense," she said, tearing off the gas receipt and tossing it in a wastebasket. "It's the rule, and I do what I'm told. Them steer-head key chains ain't real silver, in case y'all're wondering."

Marty snorted. "Think I'd think a key chain costing sixty-eight cents was real silver? Besides, I got a genuine leather one that came with my Corvette." He glanced over at the driver and spoke in a middle border between whine and threat. "I think we ought to get the owner out of bed and see if we can't change the rules and get us some fresh coffee, don't you?"

"That's all right," the driver said, giving the girl a sympathetic look. "We'll take a coupla Cokes. Marty, grab us a cold pair of Cokes."

"That'll be another dollar eighty for the Cokes," drawled the attendant.

Marty's voice came from the back of the store, near the coolers. "Good idea. Coke's got caffeine, just like coffee, don't it?"

Back outside the Amigos, Marty was complaining about how funny people talked in this goddamn-wherever place and how it goddamn made him nervous just listening to them. Bunch of goddamn hicks, that's what. A cowboy was pumping gas into a dusty pickup and looking over the Continental, walking around it in his run-down boots.

"Hey, what you think you're doing?" Marty yelled.

The cowboy looked up and smiled in a lazy fashion. "Just admiring y'all's car. What's something like this cost?"

The driver didn't know how much it cost;

it wasn't his car. Marty didn't know, either.

"Quite a bit . . . enough," said the driver.

The cowboy grinned. "Put a commode in there and it'd be a decent place to live. Must've cost more'n the house I rent over on Cholla Street."

"What you want to know for, anyway?" Marty was looking up at the cowboy, who was an easy six inches taller than the small man in the expensive suit.

"No reason, just curious. Never be able to afford one anyway on cowboy wages."

Marty hitched up his trousers. "Well, then, there's no point in asking, is there?"

The cowboy's smile was gone now, and he looked down at Marty. "Didn't mean any harm. Sorry if I troubled y'all."

His drawl was deeper and more stretched than the attendant's. He walked back to his pickup and put one boot on the running board while he minded the pump gauge running its total. At ten dollars he shut off the nozzle and hung it on the pump, watching the Lincoln move slowly out of the Amigos lot and make a right turn up San Jacinto.

"Notice we didn't have to pay before pumping the gas? Haven't seen that for a long time," the driver said. "Wait a minute, why in hell did I turn right out of the station? This ain't the highway."

"Probably getting tired, maybe," Marty said. "If they'd had fresh coffee back there, we'd be doing better. Want me to drive for a while?"

The driver shook his head, thinking Marty behind the wheel was about the last thing he needed. "No, I'll be fine. We can't be more than two hours from that place called Clear Signal. Open one of those Cokes for me while I get us turned around. . . . Goddamn, this town's got no side streets. Thought I could just drive around the block."

Marty handed him a Coke. "Shit, you're right. Vacant lot over there, use that. No side streets, are there. No streetlights, either. What kind of a place don't have any street-lights or side streets?"

"This place," the driver said as he swung left and made a U-turn, taking the Connie across part of a weedy lot. Just before all four wheels were back on the dirt of San Jacinto Street, there was a soft *pop* from the front of the car.

"What was that?" Marty asked.

"I hate to think what it was. Sounded like a tire. Give me that flashlight in the glove box." The driver stopped and got out with the light, watching the right front tire de-flate. He kicked the tire, then wished he hadn't, and shined the light on his scuffed loafer. Marty opened his door and stepped over to where the driver was balanced on one foot and wiping off his shoe with a handkerchief.

"What's wrong?"

The driver pointed at the tire with his flashlight. "That's what's wrong. Fucking flat."

"I ain't changing it," Marty said. "This is an expensive suit I got on. Wouldn't expect me to change a tire with a bad back and wearing an expensive suit, would you?"

"Well, Marty, my suit's expensive, too. So are my shoes. Now, we can just stand around in the dark and talk about the price of our clothes, or we can get the goddamn tire changed and get on with what we got to do yet tonight."

The driver took off his jacket, folded it, and laid it gently on the front seat. He rolled up the sleeves on his blue-striped shirt and tucked his tie inside the shirt. Opening the trunk, he looked over his shoulder. "Marty, hold the goddamn light so I can see what I'm doing."

"Little dusty in there, isn't it?" Marty was peering in the trunk.

"Dust is the middle name of this state." The driver unfastened the spare and yanked it out, leaning it against the back bumper.

"Jack and tire iron must be in this plastic package here."

Five minutes later, the right front of the Connie was jacked up and the driver was loosening wheel bolts.

Marty bent over, hands on his thighs. "Look, at this angle you can see the boxes taped up there on the struts. And what are we going to do for a spare if this happens again, if we get another flat?"

"I don't know," the driver grunted, fighting a tight wheel bolt with the iron. "Take a chance on getting through the night without one, get the flat fixed in the morning."

"Yeah, but what I want to know is, what if we have another flat in the meantime? Then what are we going to do?"

"Jesus Christ, Marty, will you just shut up and keep the light steady!"

Marty put one hand on the small of his back and arched forward, making a grunting sound of deep-buried pain as he did it. "Well, don't get mad. I was only asking, you know. Nothing wrong with asking, is there?"

A pair of headlights came down the dirt street toward them. Marty squinted into the lights and could see the top-heavy profile common to police cars everywhere.

"Oh, fuck, it's the cops."

"What?" the driver said, standing up with

the tire iron in his hand. He'd just taken off the flat and was getting ready to put on the spare. "Stay cool," he said. "Looks like a local. Be pleasant and don't give him any cause to be suspicious."

Marty was fidgeting as the police car swung around and came up behind the Lincoln. It was a while before the policeman got out, crackle of his radio floating over the empty street. The driver was working hard, getting the spare on and beginning to loosely refasten the wheel nuts.

"Howdy, y'all," the policeman said as he got out and walked toward the Lincoln. "Got a problem here?" He was young, maybe twenty-five, and wore a Stetson above his uniform. He also had a drawl like the cowboy's, and that irritated Marty all over again.

"Evening," grunted the driver, spinning the nuts with his fingers, beginning to sweat. Three wheel nuts to go before he could let the Connie down and tighten them up. He repositioned himself so his body partially blocked the view of the metal boxes taped to the struts.

Marty watched the officer approach them, saying nothing for a change.

The driver had one more nut to put on. He dropped it in the dirt, swore, and then said quietly, "Keep the light on the wheel, Marty, and keep your mouth shut."

"Y'all're a long way from home." The policeman flipped on his own flashlight and moved the beam over the Connie, walking around the left side and shining the light on the seats and dash.

"Yeah, we sure are, Officer. And got us a flat right here in your town." The driver was looking for the missing nut. It had rolled under the car, and he scratched around, trying to find it.

"Where y'all headed?"

"Dallas. Got business there tomorrow." The driver, having said that, suspected he'd made an error. His geography never had been very good, and he had only a general idea that Dallas was somewhere east.

"What kind of business y'all in?"

"Uh, business forms . . . paper supplies, that sort of thing."

"If y'all need to get to Dallas by tomorrow, how come y'all're not up on I-10? Ol' 90 here angles down to the river."

"Got confused, I guess. City boys aren't too good at navigating big country. I was just telling my associate here that we'd better cut back north somewhere along the line."

The officer squatted, resting his arms on his knees, and looked at the driver's work.

His Mag-Lite beam bounced directly off the metal boxes, though he didn't seem to notice them, and he canted his head as the police radio in his car chattered in the background. Marty had moved off to one side.

"Nice car y'all got here. What year is it?"

The driver didn't know; Marty didn't know.

"Company car," said the driver, still reaching under the Connie and feeling around in the dirt. "Pretty new model. Year or two old."

"Looks *brand*-new to me. Odometer says forty-three hundred miles is all she's carrying."

Finally, the driver located the lost nut and gave it a fast spin onto a wheel bolt. He was sweating through the back of his shirt, hands soiled with grease and dirt, big shoulders hunched over, and powerful forearms working the jack handle, letting the Connie down. He didn't like the cop's attention to detail.

"I need to ask y'all to show me the car registration," the officer said, his light seeming to focus directly on the metal boxes. He tilted his head and moved the beam closer in on the boxes. "Wait a minute, hold on. What's up under there, taped to the engine supports?"

The driver thought he heard another tire pop, the sound being almost exactly like that. Then the policeman slumped forward and into him, Stetson scrunched up against the driver's shoulder and Mag-Lite falling from the cop's hand.

"Jesus Christ!" The driver stood up, dangling the tire iron. "What the hell's going on?" He picked up the Mag-Lite and pointed it down. A trickle of blood was coming from the back of the cop's head.

He turned the light on Marty, who was tucking into his waistband a short-barreled revolver with a noise suppressor attached to it.

"Marty, for chrissake, what the fuck did you do?"

"He saw the boxes. You noticed him seeing the boxes, didn't you?" Marty was talking fast, almost babbling.

"I could have tried talking my way out of it, you dumb shit. He didn't have sufficient cause to do a search. Christ, now what the fuck do we do? You tell me that! And what in Jesus' name are you doing with a piece? We're supposed to have all the equipment in those boxes."

Marty didn't say anything. A porch light came on across the street, and the driver could see the silhouette of someone peering through a front window. It all seemed to be falling apart in Corvalla, Texas.

"We've got to get this son of a bitch out of sight, Marty. Quick, help me roll him in the backseat."

Marty stooped and took hold of the policeman's ankles, being careful not to get his suit and shirt cuffs dirty, favoring his bad back. The driver swung open a rear door and grabbed the front of the policeman's twill shirt, lifting him up and into the backseat.

Marty buffed his hands together, then shook them. "Told you I didn't like not having some hardware on me, didn't I? Hey, he's going to bleed all over in there, isn't he? Blood's hard to get off things. Spoil the leather upholstery, won't it?"

"Marty, shut up and do what I say before I lay you on top of that lawman. Pick up his cowboy hat and throw it in there with him. Then go back and shut off the lights and motor on the black-and-white." The driver was operating the jack, letting the Connie down on four wheels. He spun the tire iron, tightening wheel nuts. Finished, he threw the flat tire and tools in the trunk and slammed it. The porch lights across the street were dark now.

They were in the car and moving down San Jacinto toward Route 90 two blocks away. The driver's shirtsleeves were still rolled up, forearms bulging with tension. He made the left turn onto 90 and lit a cigarette as they cleared the east edge of Corvalla. "There's a pint of Wild Turkey in my bag. Get it out for me. I need a drink."

Marty turned around and leaned over the seat, unzipping a black leather suit bag. "Where is it? I can't find it."

"Top left compartment, in with my shaving kit."

"I got it. Jesus, man, the cop's bleeding all over the place now. I said that'd happen, didn't I? What're they going to say about this when we get back to the city?"

The driver unscrewed the pint and took a long hit. He replaced the cap and put the bottle under the seat. "We'll get rid of the body soon as we find a good place. Marty, you are one dumb fucker."

"Don't talk that way to me. That cop was asking for it, way I see it. And I didn't like the way he talked, anyway — what's this 'y'all' shit? Goddamn hicks. And nobody, including you, calls me a dumb fucker, got it?" Marty's voice had lost the kind of summer innocence it usually carried and had taken on a rime of dirt-gray frost.

"Yeah, yeah, I hear you." The driver started thinking about Marty's instabilities and

71

about the .32 S & W tucked in his partner's waistband.

He let the liquor take hold, loosen him, and he tried to lighten up, patching over what he'd said earlier. "Sorry. Just that we've got a mess on our hands, and I'm a little tight."

"Okay, then, long as you're sorry for saying it. *Look at that moon.*" Marty was leaning forward and staring up through the windshield. "Ever see anything like it?"

"No, I've never seen anything like it," said the driver. He hit the accelerator hard, and the Connie bored on through a night that seemed to be getting longer the longer it ran.

SEVEN

Back in 1938, Fain Bracquet fell under the heading and title of bandbox dandy. Talked like one, dressed like one in his fine suits and flashy ties with an emerald stickpin, plus little black patent-leather boots intended for fine carpet and polished floors but surely not for high-desert explorations. Ordinarily, a professional hustler would have held to a lower profile, affecting the ordinary in speech and dress so as not to rouse attention or cause the eye to notice him, but Fain pretended to be a roving salesman for the candelilla wax factories near the border and played the glad-handing "Hi, y'all, and pleased to make your fine acquaintance" role to the hilt. It was an effective cover, apparently, for who could believe someone so finely turned out and congenial would ever think of cheating at cards?

He hung around the Thunder Butte Store except for those occasions when he'd be gone for a month or two. Exactly where he went nobody ever knew for sure, but he'd always come back smiling and say things such as "Yessir, it was a profitable excursion . . . very profitable, I must admit."

The one liability in Fain Bracquet's appearance was a bad left eye, which for some reason caused him to squint and crook his head when he was looking at you. That might have come off as sinister. Yet Fain made it part of his own brand of charm, and you almost felt sympathetic toward him. He took Winchell Dear into a back room of the store, crooked his head, and squinted at him.

"Young Mr. Winchell, let's first talk about the philosophy and aims of poker, a game whose chief and undiluted purpose is to victimize others. So listen to this and write it well in the spaces of your mind where you can pull it up when called on to do so: Cruelty and deceit are two of the prime weapons of a good poker player. And, being a man, you'll find both of those qualities come more or less naturally if you just lie back and let 'em take over." Fain Bracquet wiggled his eyebrows and grinned.

"Got to play with endurance and pluck and composure, all the while maintaining an inner spirit of genteel savagery. When you're at the poker table, forget about anything resembling humane conduct [he spoke the word *humane* contemptuously, as if it were one of the worst character traits a person could possess]. Forget about friendliness, generosity, compassion, and sportsmanship. Those have no place at a poker table and do violence to the purity of the game, contaminate it, as it were. No such thing as a friendly game of poker. Try to do that, and it'll rot your skills, cause them to dull and wither. Follow?"

Winchell Dear nodded but wasn't sure he understood. What Fain Bracquet was saying ran contrary to everything he'd been taught at home.

"I see by the obvious puzzlement on your face, Winchell, that what I just said may not fit with what you've learned thus far about how to treat others. And therein lies a sticky problem, which is separating the attitudes necessary for winning at poker from those required for living decently and well the rest of the time. Some never can make the distinction. You will if you work at it. Live one way when you're not playing poker, then go another way when you sit down at the table. Takes some practice, but it can be done."

Fain let his words settle in for a moment, then went on. "One of the kindest, gentlest men I ever knew went by the name of Sailor

75

Rollins. Sailor came out of East Texas all warm and nice, like the April sun moving against the winter, but when he sat down at the table, you'd have thought a Mojave rattler was playing against you. After the game, win or lose, he'd revert to his old form and be just as sweet as you please, bouncing babies on his knee and palavering about the weather."

Winchell remembered his father talking about Sailor Rollins. Sam Dear had watched him play up in Clear Signal years ago and said it was one of the highlights of his life. "Oh, that Sailor Rollins was tough, Winchell. Made the other fellows want to fold on the first betting round by the way he played the game. As if they knew they hadn't a chance and just decided to let him have the ante without challenging him."

Fain Bracquet took out a small pocketknife with an ivory handle and began cleaning his nails, looking up at Winchell Dear between strokes and providing this: "Just remember, Winchell, in poker, and sometimes in life, there is no true and worthy gain unless there is a similar true and worthy loss by one or more of the participants. And no poker game is the genuine article unless the losers experience real pain. Without pain, you can be sure it wasn't an authentic game of poker.

76

That's why you should never play with friends when their grocery money's on the table. You following all this okay?"

Indeed, Winchell Dear was following it and wasn't sure he liked what he was hearing. All this business of pain and loss and cruelty seemed a long way from the sweet blow of Mexican wind through the chollas, the good smell of sweaty horses, and the sound of pigeon wings in willows along the river. But he figured there was nothing to lose by learning what Fain Bracquet could teach him. After all, he didn't have to play poker for a living. If nothing else, he could end up being the best campfire poker player in the Southwest if he decided to become a cowboy. Or maybe pick up a few dollars of extra spending money in the back room of the Thunder Butte Store and other such places, if he became a border patrolman. It couldn't hurt to know what Fain Bracquet knew. Couldn't hurt at all.

"Couple more things before we get started, Winchell. I'm assuming your style will be to play honest poker, perhaps as a living. You seem like a quiet, gentlemanly sort of fellow, so I'd suggest owning at least one good suit and keeping it sharp pressed; that way you're always presentable. Gray's a good color since it don't show the dust quite so bad.

"Wear suspenders instead of belts, and walk around with custom-mades on your feet, because poker games can go on for a long time, and you don't want nothing binding you and destroying your concentration. Have the boots made just a tad wider at the top, and that'll leave you room for a small handgun, something like a Colt Banker's Special. The Colt's only got a two-inch barrel, but in the poker rooms of this world we are not talking long-range, my friend. Hope you'll never need the gun, but occasionally it can get pretty dark out there on the road. Have the bootmaker sew a little leather sling on the right inside of your boot, place for the gun to ride."

Fain reached down and pulled a Derringer from his boot. "This is my backup, a forty-one Third Model Derringer. I've gotten used to it, nice and light and so forth, and the walnut grip against the brass frame is pleasing to the eye . . . to my one good eye, at least. It's removed me from peril on several occasions. But I worry that one shot might not be enough. So, in spite of my preference for the Derringer, I'd recommend something a little heavier.

"Now, let's sit down to this table here. I'm going to deal us a few hands and show you a couple of things. Your daddy says you understand straight and regular draw poker pretty well, so we'll start with those. Straight poker first, which almost nobody plays anymore, but it's good for illustrating certain things without introducing a lot of complications."

Fain Bracquet dealt five cards to young Winchell Dear. "We'll ignore the betting rounds, Winchell, and just proceed to the showdown, as if we'd completed the betting. What have you got?"

Winchell laid out five unmatched cards. "Nothing. Junk. Runt hand."

"Well, I've got a pair of fours. Not much, but I'd have beat you."

Fain Bracquet shuffled again, asking Winchell how his homeschooling was getting on and what subjects he liked best. While the boy replied, Fain dealt cards.

"Let's see what you got this time, Winchell."

"Little better, three of a kind, nines."

"Too bad, I'm holding a queen-high straight, which puts me up one better'n you." Fain Bracquet laid out an eight, nine, ten, jack, and queen in mixed suits.

Third hand: Winchell Dear pulled a jack-high flush, Fain Bracquet managed a full house, with three kings and two sevens.

He gave Winchell a whomper-jawed grin. "Sorry, kings full. Maybe your luck'll pick up as we go along, son. Here, maybe you'd like to look at my Derringer a little closer."

He broke the gun, removed the single cartridge, and closed the Derringer again before handing it to Winchell Dear.

Shuffle and deal, the fourth hand.

"Things looking any better for you?"

Winchell put down the Derringer, picked up his cards, and smiled. "Some." He laid out his cards for Fain Bracquet to see.

Fain wriggled his eyebrows again. "Oooh, four of a kind, jacks. Very nice, very nice indeed. Not quite nice enough, though." He showed Winchell spades, six through ten. "Straight flush, ten-high. Not often you see that particular hand.

"I'll deal one more hand, then we'll discuss things a bit."

Fain Bracquet swept up the cards and talked about the weather, saying things ought to be cooling down before long and didn't Winchell think so, too. Winchell agreed, said it felt that way. He also had the feeling something else was going on besides forthcoming changes in the weather.

Winchell Dear couldn't believe his hand when he picked it up. It was a straight flush, with exactly the same cards Fain Bracquet had held on the last deal.

Fain looked at him. "I haven't seen your

cards yet, but I'm guessing you feel pretty good about what you're holding, Mr. Winchell. Not much can beat your ten-high straight flush" — Winchell Dear blinked twice in disbelief as Fain laid out his cards — "unless it's a royal flush."

He displayed an ace, king, queen, jack, and ten of hearts. Odds of 650,000 to 1, and Fain Bracquet had made it.

"How you feeling at the moment, son?"

"Like I've just been run over by a Brahmer bull, that's how."

"Well, in a way you have. First off, you let me distract you by giving you an earful of mouth and showing you my gun. You were looking at the Derringer or thinking about what I was asking you and talking all the while instead of watching me shuffle and deal.

"Now, the second thing is the somewhat curious nature of the hands you received and how mine were always one better. Maybe you're a little suspicious. Would you like to accuse me of cheating? That'd be the first instinct of most folks."

Winchell didn't say anything, just sat cool and looked at Fain Bracquet.

"Son, you just did a very intelligent thing right there, keeping your mouth shut. Accuse a man of cheating at cards and tempers get high fast, oftentimes backed up by fists or knives or guns.

"Besides, how you going to prove it unless you can reach over and pull an ace out of his sleeve? Or catch him digging a thumbnail into certain cards and thereby marking 'em for later use? Only the second-rate grifters use those crude techniques. The professionals are a lot harder to spot, almost impossible, in fact. If you think somebody's got a hustle on, best thing to do is politely get up from the table and take yourself elsewhere."

"How'd you do it?" Winchell asked.

"Whoa, not so fast. You can't spot sophisticated moves until you learn the less elegant stuff the second-raters will try to pull. You don't have a stake and won't be playing in high-stakes games for a long while; high stakes and no-limit, that's where you find the true professionals, honest and otherwise. So we'll start with the basics, the vulgar stuff, the stuff you're most likely to find in small-town poker rooms or fraternal organizations or conventions of people who don't make a lot of money at their work."

From there it went on, Saturday after Saturday when Fain Bracquet was not on the road. He started off by showing Winchell what he called crude techniques, and Fain seemed to have in-the-flesh examples of each of them, which he drew from a suitcase he'd carry to the store. There were the marked cards available from so-called magician supply houses, where diluted aniline dyes were used for blockout work, subtle alterings of the floral or scroll patterns common to most decks of playing cards. Bee brand cards were particularly susceptible to alterations in the diamond shapes on the card backs.

Fain showed him how an almost indistinguishable clock-face code could be used on Bicycle brand — a nine o'clock mark for a nine, and so on. He continued on through other and more complicated marking techniques, such as sandpapering the cards, and in each case showed Winchell how to spot the markings, which wasn't all that easy to do without going over and over the cards. And once you saw them, you were amazed you hadn't seen them right off.

After that came the mechanical devices and extra pockets used to hide cards. And the small mirrors, called "glims," which could be fastened to a coffee cup or stuck in the end of a cigarette, allowing the hustler to see the card faces as he dealt them.

Fain Bracquet took his time, working his way up the trellis of cheating systems. It took him two years' worth of Saturday afternoons to exhaust his repertoire. The second year was spent on more refined approaches. Subtle moves on the shuffle, such as culling from the discards and stacking or using crimps and hops to beat the cut.

In each case, Fain was not content with Winchell Dear merely observing the technique. He insisted that Winchell become reasonably adept at the moves, not at a professional level, but good enough so he could understand what might confront him out there in the cutthroat world of poker.

"Got to get proficient at spotting the 'tells,' Winchell. That is, tip-offs, things that give away what the opposition is thinking or doing. Both cheats and honest poker players got 'em, whether it's the look and feel of the cards or the way a man holds his body at certain moments."

Some of the moves took Winchell hours of practice to get down, others took months. Second-dealing was hard, but he learned to hear the difference in sound between a legitimate top-deal and the slightly louder scrape as a second was dealt, since it rubbed against the top card and the one below it. And Fain showed him how all but the very best second-dealers would change the movement of their thumb as it pushed off a card when they were dealing seconds — the tell.

Riffle stacking, where a first-rate mechanic could arrange cards as he riffled them during the shuffle, was particularly difficult. Winchell never did master the technique to Fain's satisfaction. It became one of his personal challenges, and years later, in his twenties, he finally could do it pretty well.

Periodically, Fain Bracquet would bring up the subject of bluffing. "Not of much use in low-stakes games. Man's got little to lose, he's hard to bluff. It's only in the high-stakes or no-limit games that bluffing's got any real power. Particularly at the no-limit tables, you don't have any other choice than bluffing now and then.

"But only in the right situations, not to steal a pot with a bluff, which you might do every so often against lower-caliber players, but rather to keep people from running over you. Sometimes, even just the possibility that you might be bluffing is a good way, the only way, to keep the other fellows on the straight and narrow, keep 'em in line. If you never bluff, there's never a threat that you're bluffing. Pick your spots, however, and be careful with its use, since bluffing loses its effectiveness entirely if you try it too much and people catch on to you. And always play a bluff hand exactly as you'd play a good hand."

Then there were the bets and raises and

money management strategies. Fain Bracquet didn't seem to be very strong on these subjects, not the way he was on gaffs and hustles, and that puzzled Winchell Dear.

In circumspect fashion, he asked a question that had been bothering him. "Mr. Bracquet, if a man really knew how to play cards well, why would he ever need to cheat?"

Fain Bracquet thought for a while, and Winchell could see some combination of sadness and something else he couldn't identify across the man's face. Fain twiddled with the emerald stickpin in his tie, straightened the handkerchief in his pocket, and then pulled out his gold watch and studied it.

Finally, he looked up at Winchell Dear. "I suppose it's in the nature of some men, Winchell, something to do with pulling fast ones and getting away with it. The lift of the grift, maybe. On the other hand, maybe it's nothing more than laziness and greed.

"Son, I got to be going, need to make San Angelo by tomorrow night." He stood up and winked at Winchell Dear, then smiled and, for about the millionth time since Winchell had known him, wriggled his eyebrows. "Got a card game and a lady friend up there, and what more could a man ask for in the late middle of his life?

"Also, I think this is the conclusion of your lessons with me. I've taught you about all I can teach. You're only standing in the foyer of real card playing, and it's more'n past time for you to get in there and start playing cards for money. Nothing else I could say would be as valuable as the experience you'll acquire while sitting at the table with your best suit on."

Fain Bracquet took five one-dollar bills from his pocket. "Here's your beginning stake, and don't insult me by getting all thankful. Five dollars is a month's wages for a border Mexican and a lot of groceries for anybody in these times, so hold it close and make it grow for you. And just keep in mind what I've said over and over: When you run into an absolutely first-class mechanic, and you will, you'll never know for sure if he's cheating. But remembering what I've taught you, you'll get a sense that not all is right. That's the time to cash in and leave . . . polite but fast."

Then he laughed, tipped his head sideways, and gave Winchell a squinch-eyed look. "Be on your guard for those riffle stackers and second-dealers. Just get up and walk away, like I'm doing now. Just walk away, Winchell. There's always another game somewhere down the line."

Dust again, blowing up from Chihuahua, and a late afternoon sun headed toward the Carmens. Fain Bracquet picked up a carpet-bag valise in his left hand and gave Winchell a firm handshake with the other. "You're a fine boy. Play the cards well and straight; you'll do all right without resorting to funny business. Yessir, young Winchell Dear, you'll do all right. You're not only smart, you're also a Texan, and Texas has always produced the best poker players in the world."

He clapped a brown fedora on his head at the appropriate angle and walked through the front room of the Thunder Butte Store. After purchasing three cigars at the cash register, he stepped off the porch and headed for the lash-up serving as a one-room train station a hundred yards away, checking his gold watch as he moved along.

To Winchell Dear, the old hustler seemed smaller than when they'd first met. Part of it was Winchell's growing five inches over the last two years, and at five eleven, he was now four of those inches taller than Fain Bracquet. And maybe part of it, he supposed, was that one might always feel that way about teachers after you've learned what they know and they have no more to give you, a curious mix of affection, gratitude, and diminishing splendor. For some reason, Winchell felt a need to see him off and walked down to the station.

Cutting it close, as always, Fain Bracquet boarded the train exactly two seconds before it jerked out of the station and began chuffing north. Along with the hopper cars carrying cinnabar ore, there was a single Pullman plus the caboose. Fain Bracquet was standing on the caboose platform and waved when he saw his student watching him go.

A hundred yards up the track, blowing dust enclosed the train. But twice through the swirls, Winchell caught a glimpse of Fain Bracquet leaning on the iron railing of the caboose, looking back at him or the border or perhaps life itself. From that distance and in that moment, Fain seemed old and possessing at best a kind of tinhorn majesty, not as smooth and high-hat urbane as Winchell Dear had once thought him.

Five days and two hours later, word came down from San Angelo that Fain Bracquet had been shot and killed during a no-limit poker game. Something to do with dealing seconds, so the talk went. The talk went on to say Fain went for a Derringer stashed in his boot but never made it.

It was 1940, and Winchell Dear was just sixteen when he heard the news. The following day, he turned seventeen and went out to the flat rock, where he practiced second-dealing, kind of a tribute to Fain Bracquet and all that he was and wasn't.

And Fain had been right — when you pulled a second, the sound of the card rubbing against two other cards was far away soft as mice in the walls. But still plain and clear if you knew what to listen for.

EIGHT

When Winchell Dear acquired the Two Pair by bluffing on exactly that hand against a foolish young rancher named Rick Cobbler, the Indian had been living back in Diablo Canyon for six months. The first Winchell had heard about him came from the rancher who leased grazing rights on the Two Pair.

"You're aware of the Indian, aren't you?" Jack Stark had asked.

"What Indian?"

"Lives in the canyon at the rear of your place, six miles back. Been there for a while, not sure how long; probably's got legal squatter's rights by now, though I doubt if that's of much concern to him. Ol' Fayette or Fayette junior, either one, would have run him off, pronto, *ándale*. But young Rick didn't seem to care who came and went on the land."

"How's he get by out there, the Indian?" Winchell asked, picking up on the indirect

91

criticism Jack Stark was leveling at him.

"Don't know. I have suspicions he takes a yearling now and then. The boys tell me some eagle feathers have been turning up at the arts and crafts mall downtown, but nobody's saying where they're coming from, and I haven't noticed any Mexican eagles on the cliffs around here for some time. That might be a cash crop for him. There's no grass or water in the canyon, so the stock stays out of there, and so do I. Saw him only once, from a distance, kind of a rough-looking hombre. Just thought you ought to be aware of the fact he's back there."

In the time since he'd owned the Two Pair, Winchell had never seen the Indian. After Jack Stark had mentioned the squatter, Winchell saddled the nine-year-old paint he'd bought and rode back into Diablo Canyon, past the old La Ceila silver mine on the south slope of Guapa Mountain, the mine having been abandoned fifty years past. On his first trip, he dismounted and explored La Ceila's main tunnel into the mountain, stepping carefully along the rails where ore cars once moved and watching for snakes that favored the cool darkness of the tunnel when the white sun of June laid the desert bare and kilnlike.

Forty feet into the tunnel, a secondary horizontal shaft cut off to his right. Thirty feet farther, his flashlight caught the end of rails and the ground beneath them. Winchell squatted near the vertical shaft and dropped a stone into the darkness, straining to hear when it hit bottom, and could hear nothing. He found a larger rock and repeated the drop. This time there was the faint sound of impact after perhaps two seconds. The shaft apparently went at least a hundred feet or a little more, dropping like the stone into the belly of Guapa Mountain.

The old mine had an unsettling effect on Winchell Dear, and he retraced his steps toward the light and rode on toward Diablo Canyon. Deep in the canyon, not far from a hundred-foot-high volcanic tooth, he found a canvas-and-wood shelter roofed over with pine branches. There were signs all about that someone was living there, including blackened cookware and blankets and a freshly picked bouquet of yellow primrose placed neatly in an earthen pot, but no Indian. He called out in a friendly way, hoping the Indian might show himself. Nothing.

But every six months or so, Winchell Dear would find a side of venison hanging from the desert willow back of his house, swinging slowly in the morning breeze and starting to draw flies. Some kind of rent, he figured, and let it go at that. The Indian wasn't bothering him, he didn't need to bother the Indian.

And Peter Long Grass was content with that state of affairs. Twenty years back, not long after the mess up at Wounded Knee when the feds laid siege to the place, he'd become disillusioned with the American Indian Movement and started drifting. A longshoreman for three years in San Francisco, two years in a Nevada jail for assault with a deadly weapon when a cowboy insulted him and Peter had taken after him with a broken beer bottle, seven more as an ordinary seaman in the merchant marine. Life went on, and so did Peter Long Grass, day after day shoving back and pushing down a vague impotent fury he could neither express in words nor fully banish from wherever it lay within him.

Riding his thumb and mostly his legs down a West Texas highway thirty months ago, he'd started thinking about all the open country around him, hundreds of miles of it. He'd walked ridges, looking down into canyons, until he'd found a spot as deserted as America could offer. Near the canyon entrance was a volcanic upthrust of the kind his grandfather had talked about.

That meant water. During the far rides of September into Mexico for plunder and slaves, the Comanches had known such rocks acted as cisterns and could be relied upon in dry years. Peter Long Grass climbed nearly to the top of the upthrust and studied the crevices, judging how water might run in the rainy season. He'd traced the possible routes and on the second day found water. Eight feet up from the base was an overhang, and under the shelf was a pool two feet deep and four in diameter. Drinking from it, he smiled; the water was colder than he had expected, which meant the upthrust not only collected rainfall, but also contained a spring somewhere in its innards.

Peter Long Grass had walked the fifteen miles into town and spent most of his remaining cash on supplies. It required half a dozen trips over the next month to outfit his camp. He had no money for a weapon and could not have purchased one anyway with a felony record and identification that would not pass scrutiny. So, for a day and a night, he hunkered and poked at his fire and tried to revive everything his grandfather had said and shown him about the old ways, the making of spear and bow and arrow from the materials at hand. His recollections were flawed, but he called up some things and concentrated harder until his memories fused with distant chants his grandfather had sung, working out the technology by method and experimentation. In time, the spear was straight and the bow drew tight and the five feathered arrows were true at forty yards.

Making common cause with no one, and in the way things were said at one time, Peter Long Grass had drawn the buckskin curtain and gone back to the blanket. The old man who owned the ranch seemed not to care about him. And though Peter Long Grass cared nothing for the old man, either, it was proper to pay for squatting privileges, only and for no other reason than because it was the right thing to do. So twice each year, walking strong through the desert night, he would leave venison swinging from the desert willow near the ranch house.

He was aware of the cave on the west side of the property, near the foot of Guapa Mountain, though he did not know it was named Long Rifle Cave and was called that because of the skeleton and gun found there forty years ago by Fayette Cobbler. The entrance was a vertical drop of eight feet, but someone had placed a stick-and-rawhide ladder down to the floor. After that, the cave went on for a few yards before closing to a tunnel only slightly wider than the Indian's shoulders.

In the seventh month after having laid claim to his small piece of Diablo Canyon, Peter Long Grass crossed over the mountain to explore the cave, hoping to find an ancient arrowhead or two and thereby complete the circle he was making with his years. He searched the floor of the cave and found nothing except a rusted beer can and a plastic potato chip sack, other hunters of artifacts having already been there and having left some of their own artifacts behind.

An hour before dusk, he climbed out of the cave and began moving up Guapa Mountain. The sound of falling scree lower down caught him, and he went to ground when he heard it. A Mexican woman was coming up a trail from the foot of the mountain. She wore a serape even though the weather was still warm. At the mouth of the cave, she pulled the serape up and off, and Peter Long Grass noticed a small bundle tied around her waist. The woman went into the cave and was in there only a few minutes before emerging without the package. She brushed herself off and stood for a moment, looking around.

"Hola," Peter Long Grass said, and rose from where he'd been crouching behind a clump of desert rose.

The woman turned, drew quick air in her

surprise, and grunted as if she were about to speak, then halted speech and considered him while he considered her.

"Who are you?" she eventually asked.

"I am Peter Long Grass, and who are you?"

She continued to look at him, not breaking her gaze, saying nothing. At one time, it was clear to him, she had been handsome, perhaps beautiful. And though her face carried the lines of long trouble, only thirty pounds of weight kept her from still being attractive in the way Peter Long Grass saw things. In a certain way, she was still nice to look at even as she perspired through parts of her light dress where it pressed against her. Something about the way she held her body, some confidence in her manner as she looked at him, as if she had been around men and understood all they might think and do. That didn't bother Peter Long Grass, for he had been around many women and understood, so he believed, much of what they also might think and do.

"I am Sonia Dominguez, and I work for the owner of the ranch."

"I live in Diablo Canyon," Peter Long Grass said.

"And how long have you lived there?"

"For a time."

"Does he know you live there?" She tilted her head slightly in the direction of the ranch house, though it was around the mountain and out of sight.

"Yes, he knows."

"And you live there, that is all?"

"Yes. I hunt and gather most of what I need. What do you do for him?"

"I cook his food, clean his house."

She looked behind and beyond the Indian. "We seem foolish standing here. I have supper warming on the stove. Would you like something to eat? I live only half a mile to the east."

Peter Long Grass touched the inside of his cheek with his tongue and looked up the lower run of the Permian Basin stretching out for a hundred miles behind Sonia Dominguez. Nothing out there, no homes or other sign of permanent life. He could see a lone semi-trailer-truck moving west on Route 90, heading for El Paso or some place of no more consequence to him than El Paso.

He shifted to the woman again. "Food would be nice."

"We must wait for darkness. He can see my adobe from the main ranch house and might object to the two of us going there."

"I understand."

They sat near the mouth of the cave for nearly an hour, looking up the great dry stretch of the basin, saying little, which was not difficult for Peter Long Grass since he had lived with silence or at least its cousin for a long while, years of silence. The woman sat with her arms around her knees, serape folded neatly beneath her as a cushion. Nothing was said about what the woman might have been doing in the cave and what she had left behind in there.

There would be time for finding whatever it was, the Indian thought.

He will never find it, Sonia Dominguez thought.

She'd pointed north and east. "See that outline of what looks like a road coming around Dagger Mountain over there about five miles?"

"I see it."

"That is the remains of what is called the Great Comanche Trail. They used it on their raids into Mexico. It is said they were fine, hard riders and the most fearsome of all the Indians."

Peter Long Grass nodded and studied the trace of his ancestors.

"I wonder why they were called *Comanche*," she remarked, making conversation.

"It was a name given by the Utes — *Komàntcia* — meaning anyone who wants to fight all the time."

"How do you know that?"

"I am Comanche."

"Do you want to fight all the time?"

"No."

A few miles north, the Davis Mountains had turned blue, then purple hazed, preparing to fuse with the night.

Sonia Dominguez stood up and said, "I am sometimes lonely out here."

"So am I," replied Peter Long Grass. "It is a place designed to cause loneliness."

They walked toward the adobe, along the rim of a large dirt tank scooped out of the earth to catch runoff from the mountain. A small pool of stagnant water lay in the tank's bottom.

The woman carried the serape over her left arm and stumbled once. Peter Long Grass caught her as she took a quick step to her right for balance, near a mesquite bush. There had been an immediate sound from under the bush, like the rustle of dry leaves as they blow and twist in autumn wind.

"Stay back from that bush," he said quietly.

"Why?"

"One of our friends is under there, I think." He placed his right forearm across his chest, palm of the hand downward, and moved it away from him with a slight waving motion. "He means no harm. Like all of us, he wants nothing more than to be left alone except for those times when the solitudes become loneliness."

She looked over her shoulder as they walked past the bush. "Why do you say that . . . about wanting to be alone?"

"Not many things or people in the larger world make your life easier, and most try to take it in the other direction. A kind of wanton meanness has gradually formed out there, and I want no part of it. I have had enough of bad and have become a fugitive from the world."

So saying, he unsheathed his four-inch skinning knife and expertly cut the stems of six yellow flowers, then handed them to her. "These are evening primrose, sometimes called night candle in other places. My grandfather once told me the oils from them help to heal cuts and bruises."

He later discovered a path around the corrals that circumvented the main ranch house and did not require coming over Guapa Mountain in order to reach the adobe where Sonia Dominguez lived. That was good, because over the next two years he went to the adobe every week or so, and it would always be late when he looped around the corrals and headed for Diablo Canyon. And Guapa Mountain was a difficult climb when you were tired, when you were still feeling the effects of *sotol* and the warm, experienced softness of Sonia Dominguez, who took from you exactly what she needed and gave as much hard sweetness back to you as she took for herself. And when her breath came short and shallow, she would be saying quiet, unintelligible things.

That first night, she waited until the Indian was gone, then walked back to the cave in darkness. She lighted a kerosene lantern only when she was in the cave and used the throw of it to remove her packages from behind a rock where she had hollowed out the earth. That had been her hiding place for years, but it would no longer serve. Fifty yards west, a rock ledge jutted out. And with a spade and by lantern light, she dug back under the ledge until there was space for the packages. She wrapped them in a plastic bag and shoved them well and firmly into the space, then replaced the stones and dirt, patting the tailings flat and smooth before dusting over all of it with a cedar branch to disguise any evidence that she had been there.

Even a Comanche could not discover sign when there was no sign, she guessed. Satisfied with her work, she turned east toward the adobe.

NINE

The diamondback located the rabbit nest and found it empty. Minutes earlier, three coyotes had come by on the slink and cleaned it out, gobbling all that was warm and furry and hopeful there in the grass. They had even caught the mother rabbit, reluctant to abandon her young and staying too long and finally becoming confused by the triangulated approach of the coyotes. The diamondback hesitated, then took his seven feet in a northwesterly direction, toward the ranch house, still hunting. Sometimes there were mice in the grass near the house foundation.

Twice Winchell Dear had seen the snake. And though, in the way of most Texas ranchers, he killed any rattlesnake that happened by, this big one having lived for so many years somehow deserved to live more. As long as it stayed away from the house. Each time he'd seen the diamondback, it had been evening and along a ranch road a half mile from the house. Once, the snake simply crossed the road in front of him. He'd been on foot that time.

The second occurrence had come when he was mounted, and his horse shied well before Winchell saw the diamondback off to one side. Disturbed by the lurching horse, the snake rattled with a sound that carried for thirty yards. Winchell Dear reined in the paint and quieted her, watching the snake from well back.

"Here's the deal, old fellow. You stay out here in the desert and there'll be no bad blood between us. Come any closer to the house and I'll kill you, just as I did one of your brothers two months ago when he decided to sleep against the stone steps out front."

The horse, still afraid, snorted and tried to buck. Winchell Dear steadied the paint and from ten yards away continued to study the diamondback, now coiled into strike position, tongue flicking, rattles sounding. From the time of his boyhood, Winchell had regarded the snakes with a mixture of wariness and admiration. There was elegance about them, like the great sharks of the ocean, clean and pure in design and intent. They carried no unnecessary accoutrements or, far as he could tell, hazy dreams of random possibilities for their lives. And in the case of the diamondbacks, they meant no harm to humans unless it appeared the same might come to them.

The snake quieted for a moment, looking directly at Winchell Dear, it seemed. "Think I'll give you a name, big fellow. Maybe . . . let's see, Luther might do it. Old poker-playing friend of mine named Luther Gibbons would probably appreciate the likeness between him and you."

Winchell turned the paint for home, rode a few yards, and called back over his shoulder, "Remember our deal, Luther. Stay out here, and I'll leave you alone. Show up near the house, you'll get a load of twelve-gauge double-aught buckshot that'll make your head disappear into nothing."

Halfway to Diablo Canyon, the Indian hunkered down, troubled by the shape of what he'd seen in the last hour. He sifted dirt in one hand, cupping a mound in his palm and letting it sprinkle back to where he'd found it. Through the window of the ranch house: Why was the old man wearing a shoulder holster with a pistol in it? Old man holstered and rodded up, and the profile coming off Guapa Mountain. It smelled wrong, like a bad wind from Odessa when you could catch a whiff of the oil patch a hundred miles away as it rode the face of a blue norther.

He hurried on to his camp, lit a fire, and squatted again, letting the images form and dissolve. No conclusions, but no diminishing of the thing he felt, something to do with the half-light of an obscure malevolent presence that was up and about. If not exactly evil, then at least the absence of good, which usually amounted to the same thing in the world of Peter Long Grass. After a while, he let the fire burn down, gathered up some tools, and began to retrace his steps.

Fifteen miles east of Corvalla, Texas, the Lincoln's headlights pulled in a windmill on the left side of the road.

"I've gotta clean up, Marty, and we need to dump the cop's body somewhere. Maybe this place'll work for both." The driver swung into a short drive and stopped with the Connie's front bumper against a padlocked ranch gate.

NORTH PINTO CREEK RANCH
GATE 6, MAIN LOADING PENS
ABSOLUTELY NO HUNTING
TRESPASSING OR LOITERING

"I don't like signs like that," Marty said, peering through the windshield. "Who the fuck are they to tell me what to do?"

He leaned out the window and shouted to the driver, "Hey, don't snag your pants crossing the fence. You don't expect me to climb over that wire in this suit, do you?"

"I expect you to do just that, Marty. Somewhere along the line you need to forget about your suit and the moon and think about what it is we're supposed to be doing. Am I right?"

Marty got out of the Lincoln and shook himself, letting the cloth of his jacket drape better over his shoulders. He hitched up his trousers and repositioned the Smith & Wesson .32, checking to make sure his cuffs touched his shoe tops with no break in the crease.

"Well, I ain't climbing over that fence. What if someone comes along? If I'm out here on this side, I could say you were over there taking a piss. Wouldn't be good if both of us were in that farmer's field, would it?"

The driver had taken off his shirt and tie and was washing himself in a metal tank near the windmill. He splashed water on his face and neck and rubbed it under his arms, trying not to get any on his sleeveless undershirt. A decent roll of fat rubbered over his belt, but underneath the fat was a lot of old-time serious muscle. He could pin Marty up on one of the windmill's cross braces with his left hand and shave with the other while he was doing it, all the while whistling a happy tune as he scraped whiskers. He was tired of Marty's puling about bad backs and good suits, but he kept working on putting that aside and concentrating on the job at hand.

"You know, Marty, I'm thinking this tank's about three feet deep and eight feet across. We can dump the cop in here, weight him down, and nobody'll find him for days. Can you drag him to the fence and help me get him over it?"

Marty was making water near the rear wheel of the Lincoln. "Not unless I take off my jacket and pants first. Should've stopped by that store down the street from me and picked up one of them safari outfits before coming on this trip. Shopping in there is like going on an Africa hunting trip to the deepest heart of that country. Ever been to one of those stores?"

"Marty, shuck whatever you got to shuck and give me a goddamn hand. This whole trip is taking on the feel of an African safari."

Marty removed his trousers and jacket, folding them over the car door. He was left wearing his knee-high black socks and shoes, striped boxer shorts, shirt, and tie. He tucked his tie into his eighty-dollar white shirt and the shirt into the waistband of his shorts.

"He's too goddamn heavy. I can't get him out. You remember my bad back, don't you? Hey, what's that I heard out there?"

"I don't know. Coyote, maybe. Never heard one myself, so I'm not sure." The driver shook his head and climbed back over the fence.

The two of them, mostly the driver, got the policeman up and over the gate, dumping him on the ranch road with a thump and jingling of keys on his belt ring. Marty was carrying his Smith & Wesson in his right hand, which made that side of him useless. He struggled over the gate and dropped down to the other side.

"Jeez, we forgot about his gun. How could we do that? Look, it's a forty-four Ruger Blackhawk. Stuff it with magnums and you got a Dirty Harry boom-boom; go right through an engine block with magnums in it."

"Okay, leave the cop's gun alone — we don't need it — and find some rocks to weight him down in the water."

They hunted through the grass, finding a rock here and there, big ones, small ones.

"Think there's snakes out here? Man, I'm really afraid of snakes. Scare the shit out of me. Makes me almost puke to even think of them." Marty was talking while he located and carried small rocks. "Hate the sons of bitches more'n I hate small-town cops with a funny way of talking. They got pythons out in this country, don't they?"

"I don't think so, Marty," the driver grunted, picking up a forty-pound rock. "Those're down in the jungles. South America or someplace."

"Well, there better not be or they're done ducks. I hate snakes. Ever think what it would be like to die with one of them motherfuckers wrapped around you, staring you in the face and getting ready to swallow your head? I used to have dreams about dying like that. This ought to be enough rocks to hold that cop down in the water, hadn't it?"

They lifted up the policeman's body and rested it on the side of the tank. The policeman jerked, then let out a low, agonized moan.

"Jesus Christ, he isn't dead, Marty!"

"Oh yes, he is." Marty grabbed a handful of the policeman's hair, pulled the head back, and put a silenced round — *pop* — into where the neck joined the body. He let the policeman's head flop forward, hair

112

barely touching the water. "Now he's dead, ain't he? You bet your ass he's dead. No more of this 'y'all' shit. That's for sure, ain't it?"

The driver took a long breath, looked up at the moon Marty so admired, and flipped the cop into the water.

Marty looked over the side of the tank. "Can't see him. Can you?"

The driver began lifting rocks and placing them on the policeman's chest. After that, more rocks on the legs and head.

"Gonna scare the shit out of the first cow looks down in there, don't you think?" Marty stood in boxer shorts, skinny legs coming out from below them, and stared into black water.

"Throw his gun in there, Marty."

Far up the highway, lights appeared.

"Over the fence and into the car," the driver said. "Hurry."

While the lights were still a mile off, Marty had pulled on his pants. The driver was knotting his tie. An eighteen-wheeler came closer and then roared by on Route 90, lights washing over the driver.

Marty was already inside the car, saying, "That trucker probably thinks we're a couple of queers out here doing it."

The driver slid in and asked, "How far we got to go yet?" He turned on the overhead light and glanced at his watch. "Christ, it's after two already. We gotta get moving."

While they backed onto the highway and headed east again, Marty looked at the map. "We're all right. Another forty-five miles or so to Clear Signal, fifteen more after that. Those lights way up ahead must be Marfa. What kind of name is that for a town, anyway? . . . God, look at my shoes. Got 'em shined one hour before we left L.A., and now look at 'em."

He held his shoes up to the interior light. "Cost three hundred dollars. Ever seen such a mess?"

"Turn off the light, Marty; hard to see with it on."

"When we going to get out the Berettas? Feel better with heavier firepower in my hands, won't you?"

"When we get where we're going."

Marty was bent over, tying his shoes. "How long'll that be, you think?"

"You just said it was forty-five miles."

"That's right, I did. Not too long, right?"

"Right, Marty. Not too long."

"Then we go bang-bang and get back to civilization. Right?"

"Right, Marty. Back to good ol' L.A. and civilization, where you can't see the moon all that good, if you can see it at all."

TEN

"Winchell, you're like a goddamn creosote bush: Wherever it drips, nothing lives." Blue Griffith was pulling on his suit jacket in an Abilene hotel room.

That was Memorial Day 1967, some twenty years and a little extra before Winchell Dear would come into ownership of the Two Pair. He waved at the clouds of cigarette and cigar smoke drifting around him, trying to find a cubic foot of clear breathing space and failing. The air in the room was nearly as blue as Blue Griffith's name and state of mind.

Winchell tugged on a suspender and looked up. "How bad you hurt, Blue?"

The man shook his head and walked out the door. Winchell caught up with him near the elevator. They stood on worn paisley carpet, red at one time but blunted now to a soiled gray pink, mapped over with the stains and failings of those who had passed along it and added their signatures before moving on to other towns and greater sins.

Above Blue Griffith's right shoulder, the Texas sun was an hour up and slanting through a fire escape window thirty feet down the hall. Dust motes floated in the sunlight, and a man and a woman were arguing in a room across from the elevator.

Winchell glanced at the door, expecting someone to come tumbling out in the disarray of night sleep and carrying a suitcase, but the argument settled down, and he could hear intense low voices talking about who was going to pay the hotel bill.

Turning from the door, he asked again, "How bad you hurt, Blue? Did you get broke?"

Blue Griffith nodded and pushed the "down" button on the elevator. "After that last hand, not even bus fare." He needed a bath, a shave, and money. He needed Albuquerque and his wife.

Winchell Dear followed the custom of the best professionals and pulled out a money clip from his left trouser pocket. No mercy during the game, some afterward in the form of road money. "Will two hundred get you by and get you home?"

"That'd be real kind of you, Winchell. You know I'm good for it."

"I know that, Blue. Wouldn't be offering if I felt different." Winchell peeled two one-hundred-dollar bills from his clip and pointed his thumb toward the hotel room from which they'd come. "Roscoe McMain did the same for me in Fort Worth one time when things were going awful bad and my head got wrong. Get in these long downward slides sometimes, nothing on the deal, even worse on the draw, and you get on the tilt, start to push and chase, staying in when you know it's folding time. It happens to everybody, no matter how strong and mean you're trying to play. *Mala suerte,* as they say."

"What's that mean?"

"Bad luck."

He handed the money to Blue Griffith just as the elevator arrived. "Take care, Blue. Maybe we'll catch up with each other somewhere. Ever make it to Ruidoso for the Labor Day races? Lots of big money and low talent there. More action off the track than on it. Give you a chance to recoup."

"I don't know, Winchell." Blue leaned against the elevator door, holding it open. "I understand the technical aspects of the game all right, but I'm not sure I have the temperament for it, the heart. Some dogs don't hunt, do they? Maybe I'm one of them. Any advice?"

"Who knows?" Winchell replied, hands in his pockets and shuffling a boot toe over the carpet, looking down at it. "Guess a man's got to figure that out himself; nobody can tell somebody else about those kinds of things. My only advice is a rule I follow: If your bankroll's down, stay away from the kind of no-limit action we had last night. It's too easy to get run over. I think that might have happened to you."

"One thing I'd like to know, Winchell. Were you holding the full house I think you had on the last hand or were you bluffing?"

"I had it, Blue, filled it with my one-card draw," Winchell Dear lied, not wanting to make him feel any worse. "Had you all the way, figured you were sitting on three of a kind, at best. You did the right thing in not raising my bet. I'd have called and reraised you, right through the ceiling."

Blue Griffith stepped into the elevator, straightened his shoulders, and smoothed the broad lapels of his worn brown suit. "I didn't have anything left to raise with, anyway. You're a hell of a poker player, Winchell, and tough to hold a grudge against. Far as I can tell, you play it about as straight and hard as they come. I respect that."

The elevator doors closed slowly until only a thin middle slice of Blue Griffith was visible and then nothing at all. That was the last time Winchell Dear ever saw him. Word got around that Blue had given up poker and gone into real estate brokering. A year later, in Amarillo, Roscoe McMain would hand two hundred in twenties to Winchell.

"Blue Griffith gave me this. Ran into him in Albuquerque. He was looking pretty good and said he owed you. Said to give you the money when we crossed paths and to say hello and tell you he hoped you were doing okay."

After Blue Griffith rode the elevator down to the streets of Abilene, Winchell went back to the room where he'd spent the last eight hours. Roscoe McMain, whose waistline was about two-thirds of his height and nine-tenths of his age, resting as he did some-where in his early fifties, emptied ashtrays. Johnny d'Angelo was sipping from a glass of whiskey and listening to the radio news.

Luther Gibbons came out of the bath-room. "What do you think, Winchell? We fin-ished or what? Only four of us left, and we're all hard rocks."

"I figure so, Luther. Cash me in. Believe I'll take ship and get on over to Big Spring. Rancher north of town has a Tuesday night game starting about six. Just got time to grab some sleep, clean up, and shake myself loose to play cards again."

"Hey, Winchell . . ." Johnny d'Angelo was grinning at him. "I'm guessing you picked up about fourteen or fifteen thousand overnight, most of it from those car dealers we scared out of here two hours ago. Want to put some of it down on the Indy 500? I'll give you three to one on A. J. Foyt and his Sheraton-Thompson Special. Only four hours till race time."

"No, believe I'll let it go, Johnny. Thanks anyway."

Luther smiled at Winchell Dear. "You never bet on sports or anything other than poker, do you, Winchell? I've noticed that."

Winchell Dear smiled. "No, I don't, Luther. Just following one of the many rules my daddy laid out for me years ago."

"What'd your father do?"

"Border patrolman. But he liked to play cards." The little Colt Banker's Special had shifted in Winchell's boot. Surreptitiously, he reached under the table and pretended to be straightening his pant cuff, adjusting the ride of the gun.

"He still around?"

Winchell Dear shook his head while he organized his money into various suit pockets. "No, I'm sorry to say. Took a knife in the chest from a candelilla wax smuggler coming across the Rio Grande in 1940. Got his revolver out, but it jammed for the first and only time in its existence. A Texas Ranger blew away the smuggler five seconds later."

"Your mother, she still alive?"

"Yes. She's living on her family's ranch near Odessa. Moved there after my dad was killed and ended up marrying the top hand. They seem to have done pretty well together. I sometimes stop in and say howdy when I'm going by. Well, I'm ready to heat the axles. Anybody need a ride over to Big Spring?"

"Not me," Luther said. "I'm headed for Dallas; going to play some golf and rest for a week or two, see if my wife still loves me."

Roscoe grinned. "I think I'll walk on over to Mother Rabbit's and visit the girls for a while, see if anybody *there* still loves me."

"I've heard about that place," said Luther. "What's it like?"

"It's your basic four-get: get up, get on, get off, get out. Not much in the way of tenderness and concern for your overall well-being, of which I have a lot." Roscoe patted his stomach. "On the other hand, running around playing poker all over Texas doesn't allow a whole big amount of time for creating permanent relationships, so Mother Rabbit's is next best to simple."

Winchell Dear shrugged into his jacket. "See you sometime, then."

"Winchell . . ." Roscoe McMain was talking, hint of a frown on his face. "Be careful out there. Been a big police crackdown on poker games in some locales, and the hijackings are picking up. Two kids with shotguns knocked over that long-running game in the rear of Jimmy LeMaster's pool hall in Lubbock last month. We're all getting a little nervous."

"Thanks. I heard about the Lubbock job. One of the players apparently had been talking loud and flashing a big wad of money in the café across the street about an hour before the hijack. Stupid."

Winchell Dear went to his 1964 Cadillac in the hotel parking lot and sat for ten minutes, making notes on the game just completed. He already knew the styles and tendencies of Roscoe and Luther, and each warranted a page devoted to him in Winchell's notebook. Johnny d'Angelo was from the West Coast and new to the southern circuit, so Winchell made additional notes on him in a section of the notebook reserved for the professionals.

In spite of his sophisticated play, Johnny d'Angelo had a tell. Holding a good hand, he would look slightly away from the action, appearing disinterested. It was a common ruse and often exaggerated by poor or medium-grade players. Used infrequently, and with just the right amount of acting by a professional, the ploy could fool others into thinking the player was holding a weak hand. Winchell Dear wrote "Johnny d'Angelo" at the top of a page and made his notes:

5/30/67 5' 10", 170 lbs. Dark hair combed back, dark complexion, good suits. Adequate stake, evidently. Tough player in stud. Weaker at Texas hold 'em = overestimates his hand in terms of the flop while underestimating what other players might do with the flop. Tell on a good hand: eyes slightly to the right, disinterested, carries it off well = weak means strong. Likes sports betting. Slightly loose, overall.

Winchell Dear flipped farther on in the notebook and jotted down the descriptions of the three car dealers from Denver. They'd lost big, seven or eight thousand each. Chances were he'd never see them again, but then you never knew. Guys like that showed up, got whacked, and came back for more. He finished off with some general notes on them:

Country club players. The usual: drink too much, attention wanders, don't follow the cards well. Get looser, the more they drink. Texas hold 'em, even though they called for it, is a mystery game to them; apparently wanted to pretend they were part of the heavy Texas action. Obvious bluffers, used to buying the pot in small-time games. Harmon (last name) may try to peek at the discards; stops when he's been caught once and warned. Other two were good losers, but Harmon was not, complained and talked too much about how he couldn't get good cards, came close to insulting Luther Gibbons, twice. One of the others (Walker?) likes to "keep everyone honest" = calls even with poor or mediocre hands = makes it difficult to bluff him.

Later, Winchell Dear would copy his notes onto two sets of three-by-five cards, which he carried in file boxes. One set was alphabetized by last name, the other listed significant games and was arranged by date. If he knew ahead of time what players would be at the table, he went over his notes carefully, like any good journalist, memorizing for the short term the whos, whats, hows, whens, and whys of each player.

Winchell started the Cadillac and pulled out of the hotel lot, tipping the attendant ten dollars in addition to the ten he'd given him the night before. He liked the Cadillac to be well tended when he wasn't around it.

Down the street, two men sat in an old Chevy and seemed to be watching him as the Cadillac moved out of the lot and onto the street. Winchell Dear memorized the license plate and slipped the Banker's Special out of his right boot, laying it in his lap. But the Chevy stayed parked when he made a right turn and pointed the Cadillac toward Big Spring. Didn't hurt to be cautious. As Roscoe said, it was getting rough.

But then — he ran a finger over the thin scar along his upper lip — it had always been rough, and it couldn't get much rougher than Santa Helena on a Saturday night back in 1941, when he'd ignored one of Fain Bracquet's basic rules of survival.

After Fain died in the San Angelo shoot-out of 1940, Winchell Dear gave some more thought to becoming a border patrolman. He had just turned seventeen, time to be doing for himself. College didn't interest him, no money for it anyway, and his mother was mostly resigned to that.

Or maybe cowboying. He was a good rider,

already had some other range skills, and could learn the rest by day-handing where he could find work. Low pay and not much of a future, though. Other than that, going into the mines was a possibility, but he'd already heard the mines might be closing down before long, and miners seemed to cough a lot. Seemed you got pushed one way and got shoved another, yawing your way into life, chance more than choice picking out the routes for you.

He grinned to himself. If chance is the master, might as well be a good servant. Hell, play poker. Stop being a goddamn eunuch card wizard and start playing the game. Give it a try, at least.

He began hanging around the Saturday night game at the Thunder Butte Store, where the miners gambled, watching, studying their play. He didn't learn much. They were rough and loose and didn't seem to care whether they won or lost, playing mostly draw and five-card stud. Even though a dime ante and betting limits of twenty cents was pretty heavy action in those days for what amounted to a neighborhood game, and when you could buy a pound of coffee for twenty cents and a hotel room in El Paso for a dollar or a dollar fifty with a bath, Winchell didn't see how he could go wrong and decided to use two of the five dollars Fain had given him.

By the next Saturday night, his palms were sweating, and he rocked from one foot to the other as he waited for a seat to open up at the table. Around ten, there was an empty seat. He sat down with two dollars in change spread out before him. His first real game of poker.

The money was gone in thirty minutes. He was scared, looked as much and played that way, nervous enough that he'd forgotten most of the rules and couldn't concentrate on the game. Speculating, trying to get his money back, bluffing at the wrong times, staying in with a pair of threes when other players were calling and raising, drawing to an outside four straight with a five on top when the man next to him was showing a possible flush. Dumb, mindless play. He took out another dollar and lost that in ten minutes. Somewhere, Fain Bracquet was rolling his eyes and thinking all his teaching had been futile.

"Come again, son," one of the miners said when Winchell pushed back from the table.

Another grinned. "Thanks for the drinking money, young Mr. Dear. Thank you very much."

His father had watched the game and followed him outside. "You got to calm down, Winchell. Those boys are a little better than you might give them credit for. They drink and fool around, but some of them have played a lot of poker in their time. And don't let their jawin' bother you; that's just part of it. Tomorrow we'll go out to your flat rock and practice a little more. Consider tonight an expensive investment in your education."

The next Saturday went a little better. Winchell left the table a quarter up, and his father clapped him on the shoulder. "Any time you can walk with your stake plus something extra, it's been a good evening's entertainment."

On the following Friday, Winchell went off by himself and began running everything he knew about poker through his mind, practicing, getting it down so cold that, nerves or not, he could play a steady game. He won forty cents the next night.

It went on that way. Lose a dollar, win two dollars, drop fifty cents, win sixty cents. Somewhere, though — and this disclosed the core of Winchell Dear that would carry him through the years ahead — he shifted to a higher level of play. He lost his nervousness, began concentrating on the game.

Six weeks into the Saturday night games with the miners, he won four dollars in one evening's play. The next week he won three, and a week after he walked away with seven. At that point, the miners weren't laughing at him anymore and made sure there were never any open seats at their games.

His mother hadn't been fooled by Sam Dear's words on those Saturday evenings when he'd say, "Think Winchell and I'll wander over to Thunder Butte and see what's going on."

As she said to Winchell, looking up at the rangy young man with the thin face and slicked-back brown hair, "All you big ol' men think you're so sly and smart. I knew from the beginning what was going on down there at Thunder Butte, on Saturday afternoons with you and Fain Bracquet. Irene at the store told me. But your father assured me it was all harmless."

Nancy Dear was talking serious. "Incidentally, ever wonder where he's been drifting off to on certain Saturday nights all these years? Sam's always had this romantic idea about the gambling life. It's a fool's profession, Winchell, and that's all I'm saying, except I still think you ought to go up to Clear Signal and enroll in the normal school, become a teacher, and have a steady, honorable way of earning a living. Aside from that, I give up. You're all the same — you men —

wild and incorrigible and without the common sense God gave you."

She wiped her hands on her apron and looked out the window. "Sam's been gone three days, and I'm starting to worry. Lot of rustling and smuggling going on down near Boquillas, he said. He and some Rangers went over there on Monday."

And she knew it was bad when a border patrol truck rolled up to their place the following day. Sam Dear lay in the truck bed under a blanket. Three weeks later, Nancy moved back to the home place near Odessa and Winchell Dear became a cowboy on the R9, ten miles from where he'd grown up.

The cowboys with whom he worked didn't like the way he played poker. "Winchell, you ain't cheating us, are you?"

Winchell said, "If I wanted to cheat you, which I'm not doing, you'd never know it."

"Well, no offense, but playing cards with you is like pouring water down a gopher hole. A week's wages in three hours of playing, not to mention winning Arky's fiddle and six free lessons from him, is just too much entertainment for us, so we're asking you to drop out of our games."

At night, in the bunkhouse, Winchell practiced his fiddle and his shuffle, running through all the tricks Fain Bracquet had taught him, just to stay sharp and tight. Word got around about a serious game over in Santa Helena on Saturday nights. He was working a little north of Terlingua, and Santa Helena was a good horseback ride, fifteen miles or so. But he saddled up on a Saturday afternoon after the work was done and started out.

Traveling cross-country, he passed east of Comanche Spring, forded Terlingua Creek, and circled around the south slope of Rattlesnake Mountain. Wind and dust came rolling off the desert from the west, and as he topped a rise near the Rio Grande, off to his left he could see the Mule Ear Peaks catching a late sun.

He made the river just after six o'clock, darkness coming fast. It didn't seem like a good idea to take his prized horse across the Rio Grande, so he hobbled the gelding and paid a Mexican five cents for a boat ride. Winchell's border Spanish was good, and he asked the Mexican about what kind of town Santa Helena was.

"It is a nice village," the Mexican said as he rowed and called out, *"Buenas noches, señor,"* to a gringo mounted on a burro and splashing north across the river. Two five-gallon jugs of *sotol* were lashed over the burro's saddle.

"See the high cliffs where they split over there?" The boatman pointed. "That is Santa Elena Canyon. *Yanquis* pay for boat rides through there, but my boat is not good enough to get over the rapids farther up the canyon. There is big, mean water in that canyon sometimes. If I owned a better boat, I could earn much money taking *yanquis* like you for boat rides in the canyon."

Winchell looked down at the water sloshing around his boots and believed what the ferryman said about the boat.

A dead forty-pound catfish floated by, belly up. The boatman said whatever was washing down Terlingua Creek from the cinnabar mines killed any fish hanging around the creek's mouth.

Winchell Dear walked up to the town and studied it. He'd been told the main poker game was in a cantina on the left side of the street. Listen for the music, head that way, and stay clear of the señoritas, he'd been told. One wrong move toward the women in a village such as this meant a knife in the belly. He met several of them walking along the street, tipped his straw Stetson hat, and said, *"Buenas noches,"* but nothing more. Sometimes the señoritas said the same to the lanky young cowboy, sometimes they simply smiled, sometimes they did neither.

As he watched the señoritas, Winchell Dear's poker mind left him for a moment. They were lovely, slim and flowery, and ready, it seemed, for dancing and whatever else one did with women. That latter part had never been all that clear to him, but he had a general sense of it. He'd been thinking about women recently, after listening to the bunkhouse conversations where cowboy adventures in the cribs of Ojinaga and San Vincente were described in considerable detail.

He carried an eighteen-dollar stake plus five extra in traveling money. More money than he could have imagined a few months ago, thanks to the miners in Thunder Butte and the easygoing cowboys at the R9. Winchell Dear was playing with confidence now, developing a style that Fain Bracquet called "getting screwed down tight." Full concentration and aggressive play, blood poker.

Predators have different eyes from those of prey, something about a general sense of how the food chain stacks up, and the eyes of Winchell Dear were no longer those of prey. In his self-assurance, he'd also let Fain Bracquet's warnings slide, having decided Fain must have been exaggerating about all the cheating going on.

Things went badly at Santa Helena. Seven

men, including him, were playing straight draw poker. Winchell felt he was playing well but continued to lose on the larger pots. Two men seemed to be winning most of the big money. One was a sallow-faced little pan of sheepdip with very fast hands. The other, a big, gruff fellow with a beard and wearing a weathered gray fedora above his brown flannel shirt, was sitting to Winchell's immediate left. The place was lighted by kerosene lanterns, and in another room ten feet away, a Victrola played the same Mexican polka over and over, providing a canvas of sound for the increasingly drunken theater brought on by inclination and the night and the general pain of getting along and getting by.

Nine dollars of Winchell's stake was gone before he became suspicious that something more than bad luck was working the table. He started running the list of tells through his head, the tip-offs Fain Bracquet had drilled into him but he had put out of his mind for a long time.

Then he saw it. A right-hander dealing from the top tends to keep the fingers of his other hand curled around the deck as he deals. But the sallow-faced man's left-hand fingers dipped down, almost imperceptibly at certain times, as he pulled cards from the bottom. The signature of a less than perfect base-dealer.

Winchell played cautiously for several more hands and continued watching. The thin man was peeking and culling from the discards and placing what he wanted on the deck bottom before he dealt. The bottom cards went either to himself or the bearded fellow. By that time, Winchell was down to ten dollars and was furious. Maybe it showed.

"Well, cowboy, things aren't running your way tonight, are they," said the thin man who was bottom-dealing.

"I think there's a reason for that," Winchell Dear replied.

"And what might that be, Mr. Cowboy?" The sallow face wrinkled into a kiss-my-ass smile.

The table went silent. Four Mexicans were playing, plus the three gringos. The Mexicans looked at one another and started pulling back their chips.

Winchell pointed at the dealer and started to speak but never got it out; instead, he went violently over backward in his chair when the bearded man hit him with the back of his hand. Winchell Dear was tough and wiry from his cowboy work, but he didn't yet have a man's strength. He struggled to get up, but the big man was all over him with fists and boots.

He woke up a few hours later on the dirt behind the cantina. The village was dark, and he hurt; at least two of his ribs were cracked or broken, and he likely had a concussion as well. Dried blood matted his face, and a deep cut ran along his lip. He guessed that came from the turquoise ring the big man had been wearing on his right hand.

At sunrise he made it to the river, holding his left side and still woozy. His pockets were empty, of course, but the ferryman took him across anyway. "It is a nice village, señor, but it gets a little wild on Saturday nights. I have seen it before. You can pay me another time."

The ferryman pointed to a small boy sitting in the bow. "This is my grandson, Pablo Espinosa. He's going to be big and strong and work this hard land in the way his father does."

Twenty-one years beyond Santa Helena, and in Del Rio this time, in a saloon called the Border Dog where they locked the doors at midnight when the heavy action got under way, Roscoe McMain glanced across the table at Winchell Dear. The cards were running strange, and the smell of the game was a little shy of fine and fair. Winchell picked up on Roscoe's questioning look and shrugged imperceptibly, conveying something to the effect of, "Let's wait a few more hands and see."

He'd been studying the man sitting one player removed from Roscoe's left. Some far-back claim on his memory kept pushing at him every time he looked at the man. During a short bathroom break, the man bragged about shooting a card cheat up in San Angelo some years ago. Said the fellow was a real dandy and carried a Derringer in his boot. Winchell Dear was slumped in his chair, thumbs in his suspenders and resting, but he braced up to full inner attention at the reference to Derringers and dandies and a shoot-out in San Angelo. The death of Fain Bracquet.

Winchell folded early on the next few hands, giving him an opportunity to study the storyteller, who was now dealing. Something about the man's pallid complexion . . . and . . . and the almost indiscernible dip of his left-hand fingers at certain times as he dealt. There it was: Santa Helena. Years and extra weight camouflaged the man, but Winchell Dear now recognized him. Even the words came back from that evening: "Well, cowboy, things aren't running your way tonight, are they."

The next time Roscoe looked over, Winchell Dear nodded, and Roscoe Mc-Main launched all of his 280 pounds across the man next to him and flat onto the dealer. Winchell was up immediately and backed off, eyes flicking to each of the other players, knowing the bottom-dealer wouldn't have been working alone. A switchblade came out of a pocket, and Winchell Dear's Colt came out of his boot. The knife dropped to the floor and hands reached for the ceiling while Roscoe punched up the cheat.

"Enough, Roscoe. Let's get our money and get the hell out of here," Winchell growled.

Winchell Dear yanked the groggy base-dealer into a chair and pointed the Colt at a spot just above the dealer's nose, angry at the hustle and double angry over the fact that Fain Bracquet, in spite of all that he was not, died at the hands of this scumbag sitting bloody and beaten in the chair before him. "You pulled the gaff on me once before in Santa Helena, when I was just a young cowboy looking for a decent game, and you're not any better at it now than you were then. And by the way, the fellow you killed up in San Angelo was a friend of mine."

Winchell Dear let his eyes sweep over the other players, then stared down and addressed the dealer once more. "In the future, you look out for me, 'cause I'm going to blow your ass away if I ever see you in another card game in Texas or anywhere else."

Now these some years later he was aimed west out of Abilene, headed for Big Spring on Memorial Day 1967. In his middle forties and doing pretty well, with nearly a hundred thousand dollars in various Texas banks and ten thousand more hidden in the door panels of his Cadillac, not to mention his stake plus last night's winnings sprinkled around his suit pockets. Not bad for those days, well before the glory years of big-time poker, when you pretty much kept on the move, traveling from town to town on the southern circuit covering Oklahoma, Arkansas, and Texas. Looking for the games, the good ones, the decent paydays, all the while establishing yourself as an able poker player.

After the bad night in Santa Helena, it had begun. He'd stayed with the R9 for a few more months, got together a small stake, and then pulled out. A million miles, maybe several million, first on the buses, then on the Pullman trains, then in his own automobile when train service became thin and erratic.

You might have seen Winchell Dear over the years, somewhere out there, and probably wouldn't have paid too much attention if you had. There was nothing extraordinary about his appearance: one of those tallish thin men in gray suits with neatly trimmed dark brown hair, wearing spectacles when he read a newspaper or checked a railroad timetable. Not handsome, not otherwise. A little too thin in the face, a little awkward in his stride. Could be a banker, you'd have guessed, though the plain black boots might have seemed a little out of place in that respect, unless it was Texas or someplace like it.

Maybe you later glanced in the window of a first-class compartment and noticed him playing cards with six or seven other men. Passing time during a long train ride, you supposed, not knowing that Winchell Dear never simply passed time at a poker table.

If you had stared through the window for a moment, and not longer than that, since one of the men would have noticed the curtains were open and would have closed them in your face, you would have seen the hands of Winchell Dear work in the way of a magician's. His shuffle was fast, and he dealt with a sure, alacritous stroke, the cards streaming out like flat bullets and landing always in front of the player who was supposed to get them. By the time he reached thirty-five, Winchell Dear was one with the cards and the whisper of them across green felt.

If a player said, "I'll take three, Winchell," the cards were on the table near his hand in a quarter tick.

And you might have noticed how his face always carried the same pleasant, detached expression. He'd worked hard on that expression, practicing it in a mirror until he always knew exactly how his face looked to those who might be staring at it, looking for a tell, of which there never was any.

The road and the cards were an unforgiving lathe all their own, and over the years Winchell Dear had been turned on that device until the ragged edges of inexperience were ground and shaped. For the last year, he'd been thinking about going up to Las Vegas. He'd heard Vegas was getting better all the time, but the town was full of hard rocks all battling one another in a few games, not much in the way of mediocre players with big bankrolls, the ones always ripe for the pickings. Word was that if you were thinking about going up there, you had reason to do some rethinking unless you were plenty good and knew it. Playing head-to-head with nothing but the mean, tough boys meant a stake you put together through the years could disappear over a couple of nights in a cloud of smoke and the rank breath of *mala suerte,* no matter how neatly your best suit was pressed. Still, as Blue Griffith and others would testify, Winchell Dear was up to Vegas standards, to any standards, and there was no question about that.

The Caddy ran well and easy toward Big Spring while radio voices droned on about the race coming up in Indianapolis. Winchell turned the radio dial and found music, a good ol' Texas boy singing:

> *The guitars down the street*
> *were a little out of tune,*
> *but you could see across the border*
> *from the window of our room.*

That would be nice on a day like this one, Winchell Dear mused, to look out a window, out across the border, and have a woman sleeping in a rumpled bed on the other side of the room. That had happened one time, something like it, when he was eighteen and spent a Saturday night in San Carlos, Mexico. He'd leaned on a windowsill in the early morning and looked out toward Texas, at the Chisos Mountains just waking up.

The girl's name was Lillian, and she had been a wild young thing, aboriginal and sophisticated at once, the daughter of the R9's owner. When her parents went up to Clear Signal for a weekend on business, she and

Winchell saddled up two horses and headed for San Carlos.

He still remembered how she had been dressed: black skirt reaching over the top of her black boots, starched white blouse long in the sleeves and loose fitting, and a straw Stetson perched on black hair done up neat and fancy in the back. At seventeen, she had ridden like a Comanche, at one with the horse, as Winchell Dear eventually became with the cards.

While riding home toward Texas on that long-back Sunday afternoon, Lillian said, "Winchell Dear, y'all ought to let yourself go a little more often. Y'all're pretty good at debauchery when you lose that serious face and get to it."

She spurred the fast little mare and yelled back at him, "C'mon, let's make the dust fly and go skinny-dippin' in the river."

Before Lillian went off a few months later to Sarah Lawrence or some such place, the two of them sneaked into the canyons more than a few times. When the rains came and depressions in the rocks, the *tenahahs,* were filled with water, they splashed naked in them and made love afterward on rough creek sand. By the way Lillian handled herself when she was naked and getting down to serious business, Winchell had the clear impression he was not the first cowboy who had drifted her way and bathed in the *tenahahs* with her. After she left for college, he never saw her again.

About ten in the morning, Winchell Dear pulled the Cadillac up to a café in Colorado City. He ordered bacon and eggs over easy and looked around, thinking if such a thing as the Winchell Dear Diner existed, it would have only one stool. It was the way of his life. Until, on that Memorial Day in 1967, Lucinda Miller took his order and later came out of a kitchen in Colorado City, Texas, in a pink uniform, carrying his bacon and eggs.

ELEVEN

In the billiards room of the Two Pair ranch house, the balls sat neat and tidy, racked tightly by Sonia Dominguez as part of her cleaning chores, with the cue ball spotted at the other end of the table. Winchell Dear hung his jacket over a chair, broke the rack, ran off a string of seven straight, then let his concentration float and got sloppy. The .380 hung down from his armpit when he bent over the table and annoyed him. He removed the shoulder holster and tucked the pistol in his boot sling.

The phone rang in the kitchen, sputtered, rang again, and was silent. Sometimes it did that when there was a storm, even a hundred miles away. The wires ran long in West Texas. Winchell Dear walked to a bookshelf and removed a fiddle, once belonging to a cowboy named Arky Williams, from its case. Winchell had never been much of a musician, but the fiddle had kept him company on the road over the years. One of the six songs he knew was "Westphalia Waltz," which Lillian of his border days had greatly favored. He tuned the fiddle, switched off the billiards room lights, and stood there in the dark, playing the waltz.

Lucinda had also liked the song. But "Silver Bell" was her favorite. So he went over to "Silver Bell" and remembered Lucinda. He liked remembering Lucinda. In a life that seemed spread over with grit and smoke, the road dirt of a thousand hotel rooms, and a million poker hands, Lucinda always came up in his memory as sweet smelling and newly washed. It was after two o'clock in the high desert as Winchell Dear played "Silver Bell" for the fifth time, struggling as he invariably did with the modulations from one key to the next as the Bob Wills Band would have played it, missing a note occasionally, and all the while thinking he and Lucinda should never have let go of what they once had together.

Clear Signal, Texas, was pretty much asleep when the Lincoln Continental came down Front Street, the local name for Route 90, and stopped for a flashing red light, the only required stop on the way through town.

"Hey, look, there's an Amtrak train in the

station." Marty was pointing to his right. "We could have ridden the train out here, I bet. Could have had a compartment and played cards or something in the lounge car. No flat tires, no worries about anything. How come we didn't do that?"

The driver was watching a black-and-white move across the intersection in front of him: "Clear Signal Police Department, To Protect and Serve." He gave the car plenty of time to get farther in the direction it was headed before pulling away from the flashing red light and continuing east.

"Amtrak's puffing out, going the same way we are. How come we didn't ride the train?"

"I don't know, Marty. Didn't think about it, I guess. Besides, trains don't give you the kind of flexibility we need. Look, we've only got about fifteen miles to go. Check that hand-drawn map we were given, one more time."

Marty unfolded the piece of paper torn from a legal pad and squinted at it. "Yep, fifteen miles is what it says. We better be thinking about getting the equipment off the engine struts and into our hands."

"We will, soon as we get near to where we're going."

The Connie went past a saddle shop, past the Sonic Drive-In, past the Cholla Bar with plywood over the windows and cowboys in the parking lot, drinking beer near their pickups. The cowboys turned and watched the Connie slide past them, looking faintly bellicose with their hats pulled low and faces in shadow.

"Pretty mean-looking bunch there in the parking lot," the driver said.

"Yeah, one burst from the Berettas we've got riding on the struts and they wouldn't look so mean, would they?" Marty turned and watched the cowboys watching the Lincoln.

Past a line of motels, the Best Western's marquee reading, "Welcome Film Crew."

"Hey," Marty said, "they must be making a movie or something out here, probably a Wild West thing. I hate being in this country, but I like watching movies about it. Always laugh when I see some movie cowboy guy shooting a forty-four and holding it like a cap pistol. Son of a bitch'd jump right back and crack him in the face holding it like that. Ever watch those old cowboy movies they run this time of night?"

"No, I keep pretty regular hours most of the time except when I've got one of these jobs to do. Got a family, you know."

"Your wife and kids know what you do for a living?"

"They think I'm a salesman. That's what I tell them. My wife's a little suspicious, always has been about that line, but I bring home the bacon and she doesn't say much. Told her I sell secret computer parts and can't talk about it because of industrial piracy problems."

"Glad I'm not married," Marty declared. "Too many worries being married. All I got to do is drift down to the Orchid Lounge over on Vine and pick up a little something when I get the urge. No worries other than that. Got naked dancers there, too . . . at the Orchid. Some of the hugest tits you're ever going to see. For a tip they'll sit on your lap and shake 'em right in your face. That's kind of fun sometimes. Ever been there?"

"No." The driver clicked the headlights up to bright as they moved past the Buckin' Bronc truck stop and beyond the city limits of Clear Signal.

"Damn, the moon's gone. All kinds of clouds up there." Marty leaned forward and looked up through the windshield, then pivoted in his seat and tried a side-window view.

"Yeah, wind's come up, too," the driver said. "Feels to me like the temperature's dropping."

"I didn't bring a topcoat, did you? Didn't

think about that. Hell, this is still August and you wouldn't think about needing a topcoat. Got a beauty I picked up on sale over on Rodeo Drive, direct from Savile Row in London, they said. Cashmere, pretty close to the nice cream color of this car. Should've brought it. Didn't guess it would get cold on us, did you?"

"No, never gave it a thought. The sign on the edge of Clear Signal back there said the elevation was forty-seven hundred feet. I suppose the weather's a lot different out here. . . . Jesus, that wind's really picking up, can feel it even in this heavy car. Ten more miles and we're ready to go to work."

"Then back to civilization where you can't see the moon, right?" Marty laughed. "I'm going to miss seeing the moon like it looks out here, but that's all I'm going to miss about this place. Should've brought my topcoat, though, don't you think?"

The driver slowed the Lincoln and pulled into a roadside park. "This is about right for getting the equipment ready."

"Hey, I don't want to get my suit dirty getting those boxes down from the struts."

"Don't worry, Marty. I'll take care of it. I've become more and more aware of your suit during this trip."

"Well, hell, I don't want to appear uncooperative. Just don't want to mess up this good suit, you know. Can't blame me for that, can you?"

Dark clouds moving fast across the sky and wind blowing empty plastic cups across dry grass as the driver halted the Connie.

"Look, a goddamn tumbleweed. Just like in the old movies." Marty was excited, pointing at the tumbleweed racing past the car, through the headlights, and into the darkness.

The driver was out of the car, wind flapping his coattails, calling for Marty to hold the flashlight while he unfastened the metal boxes.

"Jesus, goddamn wind's something else, ain't it? Not as cold as I thought, though. This wind, spookier'n shit, don't you think?"

"Marty, point that light up under here for me."

"Damn hair's blowing in my face. Should've brought a hat or something. You bring a hat?"

"Hold the light steady, Marty."

The driver reached up toward the engine struts, being careful not to touch anything that might be hot. He found the boxes and fingered along them, feeling for an edge of duct tape he could use to peel the rest away. A section tore loose, and he handed it to

Marty. Another section, then a third, and more after that. The boxes loosened until he could grasp the end of one and yank on it. One box came into his hand with strips of tape still clinging to the metal. The other was dangling, held only by a single piece of tape still attached to the strut. It came off and out with a single jerk.

Marty's left hand was full of oil-soaked, sticky duct tape. He whipped his hand about, trying to dislodge the tape. One piece stuck to his shirt cuff, and he shined the light on it. "Jesus Christ, what a mess. Look at this shit; got a greasy, sticky spot on this eighty-dollar shirt. Ever see such a mess?"

"You packed solvent for cleaning the weapons, didn't you? It'll take the sticky stuff off your hand."

"Yeah, but not off this eighty-dollar white shirt. Not even sure my Chinese laundry buddies can get the spot off the shirt."

Back in the car, the driver opened one of the metal boxes while Marty held the flashlight. The Beretta 93R lay quietly on red felt in its own section of the partitioned box. The pistol had a wooden butt and a folding metal grip attached to the front of the trigger guard. With the grip in its down position, the forward hand could take hold of the grip with the thumb hooked in the extended trigger guard, thus allowing a two-handed hold on a relatively small weapon. Stamped into the barrel support was "PIETRO BERETTA Gardone V.T. Cal. 9 Parabellum," the word *parabellum* coming down from the Old Latin and meaning "If you want peace, prepare for war."

In a separate section of the box, three twenty-round magazines containing nine-millimeter cartridges were stacked. And in yet a smaller section were cleaning tools and solvent wrapped in plastic.

"Man, look at that." Marty was grinning. "One of the prettiest guns you're ever going to see. Ever use one of these?"

"Not this exact model. I'm familiar with an older model, the M9 fifty-something."

"That was the M951, which was followed by the Model 92. This is another improved version of the old 951."

"This the rapid-fire lever, here?" the driver asked, lifting the pistol and testing the heft and fit of it in his hand, pointing at a thumb switch with the other hand.

"Yep. Flip the lever, and the gun changes from single-shot to firing three-round bursts, which is just about optimum. Any more on full automatic and she'd begin to wander on you. Plus this model's got a compensator" — Marty put his finger on an open-ribbed portion of the barrel at the muzzle end — "blows gas upward when you fire, which pushes down on the gun. Counteracts the tendency of the muzzle to rise when you're in rapid-fire mode. Man, they sent us with first-class equipment."

"They always do, Marty. Remington pump shotguns the last time, remember?" The driver shoved a clip into the pistol, folded down the metal handgrip, and aimed at an imaginary target through the windshield. "They were afraid we might run into a bunch of ranch hands on the property, so that's the reason for the Berettas."

Marty opened the second box and took out his pistol, imitating what the driver had just done. "Shit, better wipe off this crap from my hand 'fore I get the little honey all sticky." He opened the plastic package, poured solvent on a gun cloth, and cleaned his left hand. Outside, the wind was gusting near thirty miles an hour, blowing dust and beer cans across the roadside park.

The driver laid his pistol on the seat beside him and began to pull out of the park. Marty was now full in his element, a world he understood and in which he was competent.

"Man, oh man, I just love holding machinery like this. Get caught with one and the BATF will haul you off and make you spend half your life in jail or something." He swung his Beretta in a slow arc, pointing it toward the road in front of them: *"Dah-da-dah . . . dah-dah-dah . . . dah-dah-dah.* Won't take long to get our work finished with these babies, will it?" He wiped off the already immaculate gun with a corner of the cloth he'd used for cleaning his hands, being careful not to get any sticky residue on the pistol.

"Five miles to go, Marty. Should be coming up on that place called Slater's Draw pretty soon."

"Can't wait," Marty said, putting down the gun and straightening his lapels, brushing the sleeves of his suit jacket with his hands, examining the smudge on his shirt cuff one more time. He was already feeling a little hungry.

Lucinda Miller was a Texas woman from up near Muleshoe, the flat-ground country called the Llano Estacada. She wasn't what you'd have called pretty, back when Winchell Dear met her, but then and on the other hand, she wasn't anywhere near the opposite extreme. One of those women who start out plain as a young girl and grow into something with a certain look and style that, on close examination, gives promise of more than an offhand glance would suggest. The kind of smile certain women develop as they grow older, a special way of holding their bodies and talking with an easy laugh behind the voice. As if the world has done about all it can do to them, and anything out in front is bound to be an improvement, or at least no worse.

Lucinda had set bacon and eggs before Winchell Dear that Memorial Day in 1967, a day that already was warm and gave all indications of heading toward hot. The roadside café in Colorado City, Texas, didn't have air-conditioning, and the saltshakers had rice in them to keep the humidity from clumping the salt. There were flies on the screens and on catchfly paper dangling from the ceiling on strings, twirling slowly in the breeze from a large fan near the door. Winchell Dear removed his suit jacket, folding it on the empty stool beside him. It was after breakfast and before lunch, so the place was mostly empty except for a group of four paying their bill.

After ringing up the bill, making change, and thanking them, Lucinda Miller walked back toward where Winchell Dear was buttering his toast.

"Like jam for that? We have some orange marmalade."

"That would be real nice," he said, liking

the easy laugh only just hidden behind the woman's voice.

She fetched a jar of marmalade from farther down the counter and put it in front of him.

"You from Colorado City, here?" he asked, taking a sip of hot coffee, black and good, feeling a little out there by himself and tired of talking to poker players.

"Now I am. Originally from up near Muleshoe. Then Lubbock after that for a few years, birthplace of Buddy Holly."

Winchell Dear looked puzzled, poker face gone now that he wasn't at a table somewhere. "Don't believe I've heard of . . . who was that? Buddy . . ."

Lucinda Miller laughed straight out. "Hey, mister, where you been? Before he and Ritchie Valens and the Big Bopper crashed in a private plane somewhere up in the winter wastes of Iowa, ol' Buddy was almost as big as Elvis. You know, 'Every day it's a'gettin' closer. . . ,' " she sang in a pretty fair alto.

"Sorry . . ." Winchell Dear grinned. "Doesn't ring a bell."

"You need to put a little more music in your life, hombre. Learn to play something, go dancin', all that."

Winchell chewed on a piece of bacon, done crisp just the way he liked it, then reached over to the paper napkin container, pulled out two, and wiped his hands and mouth. "Now you're jumping to conclusions about me. Matter of fact, I play the fiddle a little bit. Know six songs, working on a seventh — 'Great Big Taters in Sandyland' — haven't got it down yet, don't know if I ever will. Doesn't matter, six songs are enough to get by on in life, if you really like those six songs. Come to think of it, one good song would be enough, if it was really a good song and you really liked it."

Lucinda tipped her head, got a crooked smile going, and said, "Now *that's* a pretty profound statement for a hot morning in the latter part of a month called May . . . one good song is enough. Like that idea, got to remember it when I need a little boost, of which I need a little a lot of the time. Play the fiddle, huh?"

A truck driver pulled up out front with a *whoosh* of air brakes and came in, taking a seat four stools down from Winchell Dear.

The man coughed hard, covering his mouth with a closed fist, then opened a menu.

Lucinda walked in the man's direction, saying, "You okay there, Ralph?"

"Howdy, Lucinda. Good to see your smiling face again. Yeah, I'm okay, got me a little shippin' fever or something in the chest; won't seem to go away and leave me alone. Don't know why I even bother to check the menu, already know what I want."

"Let's see if I can remember," Lucinda said, folding her arms and rolling her eyes up toward the fly-specked ceiling. "Ralph, drives a semi for Seminole Lines, comes in every couple of weeks, and always orders . . . three eggs hard fried, tall stack of buttermilk cakes, one tomato juice, and a side of ham. Coffee makes his stomach jumpy, so he just sticks with tomato juice. Right?"

"Lucinda, you're a natural wonder. You ought to enter one of them TV contests where memory's important."

Lucinda wrote on her small green pad, tore off the order, and plopped it on the high counter separating the kitchen from the rest of the café. A disembodied, hairy male hand clutching a lighted cigarette grabbed the order, with the sound of batter hitting a hot griddle coming a few seconds later.

"Want a copy of the *Odessa-American* while you're waiting, Ralph?"

Ralph nodded, and Lucinda slid the paper along the counter to him. She walked back toward Winchell Dear, who was swallowing his last piece of toast and washing it down with coffee. He took another two paper nap-

kins and wiped his hands while Ralph of
Seminole Lines unfolded his spectacles and
bored in on the latest news.

"So, what do you do for a living, mister?
You a traveling man or something?" Lucinda
Miller was smiling at him.

Winchell Dear never made noise about
being a professional poker player. Not that
he was ashamed of it; a living was a living,
after all, and his way of getting by was as
honorable as the next, long as you played the
game hard and fair. That's how he saw it,
that's how he lived it. But somehow, if you
told people you played poker as a business,
they'd look at you as if you might grab their
underwear and run, after which the conversation was likely to shift into poker strategy
and what did Winchell Dear think of drawing to an inside straight and the like, none of
which he cared to explain.

So he was about to offer his usual line of
talk about being a gun and ammunition
salesman. He knew enough about guns to be
reasonably persuasive unless pushed too far.
But he was never in one place long enough
for anyone to get beyond the basic rifle and
shotgun questions, and he read one or two
gun magazines each month just to keep the
nomenclature in his head.

Before he could answer Lucinda Miller's

question, Ralph of Seminole Lines turned from his paper and looked over the top of his reading glasses toward Winchell Dear.

"I'll tell ya what that gentleman does for a living, honey. Thought I recognized him when I first came in, but it required a second look before I was sure. He's a professional gambler. Watched him play once at a truckers convention a few years ago. He must have walked away with ten thousand from a weekend's work. I remember because my boss was playing at his table and said the man was either cheating or the best poker player he'd ever seen. So I sat and watched him play on two different occasions and decided my boss was right. This gentleman here'll just grind you down to road tar and leave you stuck to the pavement."

Lucinda Miller canted her head again. Winchell thought it was real attractive, the way she did that and how she smiled her little crooked smile at the same time. "Well, well, a real true-to-life gambler right here in front of me. Ralph correct on that?"

Winchell Dear sipped his coffee, annoyed by Ralph's recollections and assessments. "No, I play poker for a living."

"That's gambling, isn't it?" Lucinda asked.

"Depends how you look at it and how you play it."

Ralph couldn't resist the opening. "You play straight, right? My boss figured you did, said at least he couldn't catch you at anything, and my boss is a pretty observant fellow."

"I play straight," Winchell Dear said, giving Ralph a sharp glance. "No need to do it any other way if you know what you're doing." He was also pretty sure he could riffle-stack and bottom-deal Ralph's boss into bankruptcy, if it came down to proving something.

"Well, probably beats driving a truck for a living," Lucinda Miller said. "Use your brain instead of your arms and butt. Right, Ralph?"

Ralph went back to his paper, then picked it up and moved to a booth in the far corner of the room, as if Winchell Dear carried something infectious.

Lucinda glanced at Ralph's fat rear walking away, smiled, and shrugged. "So, where you headed next, gambler?"

"Big Spring." Winchell Dear usually didn't tell anyone outside the profession where he was going, but somehow he felt like telling the tall woman. "Kind of hard to ask this — not my nature to be forward — but you married or otherwise tied up in a similar way?"

The tilt of the head again, the smile again.

"No. My husband was in the air force till his cargo plane went down on a training mission over at Reese AFB by Lubbock. Wasn't much left to bury. That was two years back. I came down here six months ago and been going to night school over in Sweetwater, learning how to keep books and be a legal secretary. Plopping bacon and eggs in front of locals and drifters isn't all that challenging. You got a reason for asking about my marital status?"

"Well, thought I might ask you out for dinner sometime if you're at all interested in having a so-called gambler for a dinner partner. I don't flip coins or play liar's poker for the check, in case you're wondering."

Lucinda Miller folded her arms and looked straight at Winchell Dear, a look worthy of a first-class card player giving the once-over to a stranger who had just sat down at the table. He appeared to be all right, a decent package in a plain wrapper. No Clark Gable or anything close to it, but neatly done up in a nice dark suit and well-barbered hair, thin in the body and eyes sagging a bit, good strong nose and chin. Looked like he could use a shave and a little sun, though. And she liked his blue suspenders.

A gravelly voice sounded from the kitchen:

"Eggs, cakes, and ham up."

While Lucinda delivered Ralph's breakfast, Winchell Dear stood and walked to the cash register with his check, reaching for his billfold.

Lucinda returned and met him on her side of the register, took his five-dollar bill, and handed change back to him. "Since you're asking, I'd be pleased to have dinner with you. Don't get invited out much here in Colorado City. But it'd help to know your name."

When he told her, she reached out and shook his hand, saying, "I'm Lucinda Miller. I go to school on Monday, Tuesday, and Wednesday nights. Other than that I'm a free woman. Got a preference?"

"How about Thursday? Need your address and phone number . . . uh, so I know where to pick you up. Seven o'clock about right?"

"Just right." She scribbled on the back of a green order ticket and handed it to him. "There you are, name, address, phone number."

"See you Thursday evening, then." Winchell Dear smiled at her and shoved his billfold into his left hip pocket.

"By the way," she said, "we going low down or fancy or in between? Just so I know what to wear."

"Big Spring's got a couple of nice places if you don't mind the ride. I guess by West Texas standards, they'd be called fancy, so let's go fancy."

"Fancy it is," Lucinda Miller said, that pleasant laugh lying just behind her voice.

Winchell Dear backed his Cadillac out of the café lot and pointed it again toward Big Spring, feeling better in some indefinable way than he'd felt for a long time, as if maybe the music hadn't died with the untimely passing of someone called Buddy Holly.

So it came, twenty-three years after Memorial Day in 1967, Winchell Dear stood in a darkened billiards room and played "Silver Bell," remembering Lucinda. The wind had risen quick and hard, as it often did in the high desert, and the blow of it rattled the French doors on the south wall of the billiards room.

Across the room, beyond and below the French doors, seven feet of diamondback rattlesnake moved slowly along the ranch house foundation. The snake was not angry or sad or frustrated or afraid. The snake was hungry, that was all. Yet, as is characteristic of *Crotalus atrox,* its behavior carried the symptoms of an edgy and nervous temperament.

Somehow aware of rising wind but deaf to

the airborne sound of a fiddle playing "Silver Bell," the diamondback hunted on through the night, alone and black eyed and searching. The tap of a fiddler's boot on a wooden floor was transmitted to a cement pad below the floor and thence to the ground below it. Stopping then, the snake rose and stared through the French doors, tongue flicking. Whether it could see Winchell Dear standing in darkness and looking in its direction was not certain, but the snake soon returned to its hunt, moving past the doors and along the foundation, alert and ready for whatever might come its way. And, as before, the diamondback was not angry or sad or frustrated or afraid. The snake was hungry, that was all. And a little edgy, in the way of its nature.

Winchell Dear adjusted the .380 in his boot and took up his fiddle again, playing this time the song a Las Vegas musician had written about him, humming some of the words as he bowed and fingered:

> *. . . as all we dreamers know,*
> *it's not the winning it's the game.*
> *We all stay the same,*
> *it's just the dreams that get older.*

TWELVE

Peter Long Grass circled the foot of Guapa Mountain until he was due west of the main house and a hundred yards north of the place where Sonia Dominguez lived. He climbed two hundred feet up the shallow slope and settled himself. From there, he could see both the main house straight down from him and the rough outline of the woman's smaller, darkened building off to his left.

Why he had done this, had gathered up his tools and jogged through darkness to sit on the side of Guapa Mountain, he still wasn't certain. Though anyone who has ever awakened to the sound of banging shutters or an imagined footstep in the hall might understand what had brought Peter Long Grass across the night to this place of watchfulness. We all are yet driven by old fears and the sound of creatures unknown snuffling around the cave mouth, held in abeyance only by the wall and the fire and the weapons beside us. And, therefore, so was Peter Long Grass.

And something was out there, something incalculable about this night. The smell of the wind as it had risen and swept the land in the last two hours, bringing with it an indistinct, lingering ambiance of all the bad Peter Long Grass had tried to leave behind. Given only that much, and *only* is sometimes enough, he had come to defend whatever he now had, even if it was merely a wood-and-canvas shelter in Diablo Canyon. But there was more to it than rock and stone and wood and canvas. The woman, Sonia, and the old man, Winchell Dear, and he, Peter Long Grass, had reached a kind of equilibrium out there in the high desert, and he was determined to preserve what passed for contentment in this time of his life. For Peter Long Grass, there was simply nowhere else to go.

Perhaps none of what he felt there on the side of Guapa Mountain was real; perhaps the night would pass and the dawn would come and the day would bring nothing more than the ordinary. If so, he could look back and smile at his fears. For now, he assumed the role of prudent sentry, a one-man picket line in the windblown cedar and mesquite of the high desert.

A group of javelinas drifted toward him, snorting as they rooted and grubbed. At fifteen feet he gave them a low, sharp "Hah!" and the pigs crashed off through the underbrush.

In the adobe, Sonia Dominguez turned in her bed and looked at the clock beside her. She was tired from the day just passed and even as tired from the restless sleep she'd passed through in the last three hours. It was three o'clock, and the alarm would ring in another half hour. On the other side of her bedroom door, Pablo Espinosa snored loudly enough almost to override the sound of night wind whining through the cedars, the wind sometimes close to the sound of a woman's scream as it found the cracks where her windows were not properly fitted.

She lay down again and let her thoughts run. Often, as they did in these morning hours, her thoughts went to the baby she'd given up at fifteen. The young San Diego sailor she had loved was handsome, and in the few days she had known him, she'd been fascinated with the contrast of his red hair and light freckled skin against the black and brown of hers and had found in that a kind of eroticism all its own. The boy-child would be into his thirty-eighth year now, and she wondered if he had grown to be as large and strong as his father had been. She remembered the young sailor's muscular forearms and how he'd walked on the biggest feet she'd ever seen — size EE and length thirteen. He'd told her that when she'd asked, and it was one of the many random things she carried in her memory.

When she'd last written to find any news of her youngest son, perhaps thinking she might at least send a letter to him, she'd been put off by what relatives still remained in Los Angeles and told only that he had a nice family and was doing well as a salesman of computer parts. And on this night, as was true of many nights, she wondered where he went and how he went and if she would ever see him again.

The driver slowed and let the Connie roll nearly to a stop before touching the brakes. The headlights shone on the bridge sign ahead of them: "Slater's Draw."

"Okay, this is it," the driver said. "The ranch gate is supposed to be another mile or so farther on. Read me those notes again at the bottom of the map."

Marty again unfolded the sheet of paper they'd been given, using the flashlight to study it. "Says there are two houses on the place, and our target'll be in the adobe one a

170

little way from the main house. What the hell is adobe? Some kind of cement or brick or something, ain't it?"

The driver moved the Lincoln slowly along Route 90, looking for the ranch gate. "Yeah, I think so. Kind of an old-fashioned cement block, I think."

"How we gonna tell adobe from cement or whatever in the dark?"

"I guess we'll use our flashlight, Marty, unless you got a better idea. Hey, here we go." He turned right, pointing the car into the beginning of a ranch road. The headlights illuminated an iron ranch gate with two "NO TRESPASSING" signs on each side.

"What's the lock, Marty?"

"It's electronic. Can't pick it 'cause there's nothing to pick. I can probably disable it with a burst or two from the Beretta."

"I don't think so. You might blow up the lock all right, but that bar running into the post is just going to freeze in place. Besides, too noisy, too messy."

Marty pulled out the handwritten map one more time. "I ain't walking, if that's what you're thinking. Not across this goddamn desert in these good shoes, in the dark with the wind blowing like a hurricane. Not thinking of doing that, are you?"

"Marty, we'll do what we have to do to get

the job done. It's not any more complicated than that. I remember something else on that sheet of paper, something about another entrance. What's it say?" He leaned forward, resting on the steering wheel, wondering how long they had until first light. The flat tire and then killing the policeman and putting his body in the tank had cost them over an hour. His watch showed the time was nearly 3:30.

"Down at the bottom here it says there's another entrance a half mile farther east. Got to turn left first, then circle back south under the highway and a railroad trestle. Says, 'Old unlocked gate near the trestle.' Guess people aren't supposed to know it's there."

"My God, this is becoming a damn nightmare." The driver let out another of his long breaths and wiped the palm of his left hand across his face. "Let's try the alternate entrance. We've got to get a move on, though."

A semi rolling hard and fast through the Texas night screamed by them, heading east.

"Look, way up there by that mountain —" Marty pointed. "I think I can see house lights barely twinkling through all this brush and cactus and shit. Suppose somebody's up and around this time of night?"

"Might be yard lights of some kind. Farms

have those." The driver went back on the highway and accelerated.

"This is a ranch, not a farm, ain't it?" Marty was holding his Beretta on his lap, coming up to his killing state of mind.

"Ranch, farm, all the same far as I'm concerned," the driver said, slowing again and making a left turn off the highway, steering the Connie down a dirt track just short of a railroad trestle. As instructed, he followed the track where it circled back under Route 90 and then under the trestle, bringing them to another gate, which was nothing more than framed wire.

"Check it out, Marty, and hurry."

Marty got out of the car and stepped into a fat stand of prickly pear cactus growing and spreading over two square yards. "Jesus! Goddamn, I'm hung up in thistles and shit. Man, do they hurt, poking right through my good suit pants, too. Think I ripped my pants."

"Hurry, Marty. We're running short of time. Be first light sometime before too long."

"Just a minute, goddammit. Got to get out of this fucking briar patch." Pointing the flashlight down, he gingerly extricated each thorn from his skin and pants, then rolled the trousers up to his knees and minced sideways out of the cactus and toward the gate.

By now, the driver's palms were sweaty. This was his operation to manage. Marty was the main triggerman, and the triggerman looked like some kind of circus clown out there in the headlights with his pants rolled up and his coattails flapping in the wind.

Marty unfastened a length of chain and dragged the gate back toward the Lincoln. "Think I should close it after you take the car through?" he shouted over the wind.

The driver leaned out the window. "No. Leave it open; we'll come back out this way. I'll pull up a little so you don't have to fight the cactus again."

Back in the car, Marty picked up his Beretta, cradling it in his lap. "Let's get this fucking job done and get the fuck out of Texas. I've about had it, haven't you?"

"Yeah, I sure have. Now all we got to do is find the house. I can't see any lights from where we are now. Now, the highway curved a little southeast before we hit the trestle. We turned approximately north off the highway, then came back south under the trestle. That means the house should be somewhere between straight ahead and off to the right. Not being able to see any lights, I figure we must be on the down side of a little slope, with the house on the other side of the slope. Maybe a mile or two away."

The Lincoln bumped and bounced over the rocks of a ranch road angling in the general direction the driver wanted to go. "Should douse the lights, but I can hardly make out this road as it is. Jesus, listen to the scrapes — sounds like this brush is taking paint right off the car."

From his place on the side of Guapa Mountain, Peter Long Grass had seen car lights stop by the main ranch gate. He watched them as they moved farther east along Route 90 and turned back under the Southern Pacific trestle. And now the lights were coming across the desert toward where he sat just above the main ranch house. He stood, gathered his tools, and began quietly descending Guapa Mountain, stopping every thirty feet to check on the position of the oncoming vehicle.

When her alarm went off at three-thirty, Sonia Dominguez rose and put on her bathrobe. Pablo Espinosa was sleeping on the blanket in her kitchen.

She shook him awake. "Get up, old man, it's time for you to go."

"It is still night," mumbled Pablo Espinosa. "I go at first light; I am weary of stumbling through darkness."

"I will make coffee and cook eggs for you. I want you over the ranch boundary and on the highway by first light. It is an easy walk west along the road and then turn north when you come to the western fence line."

"I have done it before." Pablo Espinosa struggled onto a chair and rubbed his eyes with the knuckles of both hands. "I need to use the toilet."

"Go use the toilet, then. The blue towel I laid by the sink is yours."

"I think I still have a fever."

"Your fever will be gone when you get back home. If things go right and *la migra* gives you a ride, you'll be there before sundown."

Ten minutes later, Pablo Espinosa sat again at the kitchen table of Sonia Dominguez. He ate tortillas and eggs with salsa spread over them. The coffee was strong and black, too strong and too black, so he asked for a little milk and sugar.

"Old man, you must drive your wife loco with your whining and your demands. Do you drive your wife loco?"

"No, my wife loves me and knows how I take my coffee."

Sonia Dominguez looked out a living room window and saw lights in Winchell Dear's house a quarter mile away. The old man must be staying up all night; he did that sometimes. She glanced toward the east, where dawn was coming up on Tallahassee, Florida, and was running hard toward West Texas.

Thirteen

As the Lincoln mounted a rise, the lighted windows of a ranch house were visible only three hundred yards away. The driver cut the headlights and stopped. "I think we walk from here, Marty. I can't see where I'm going without the lights, and I can't leave them on any longer. We'll take the guns and flashlight, leave the car here."

"Aw, for chrissake —"

"Don't argue," the driver interrupted, voice tense and sharp, out of patience and out of time. "This job is my responsibility. You're the shooter, I run the operation. And I say we walk from here. Locate the target, do the work, and we'll be back in El Paso before lunch. Find a good hotel, get something to eat and some sleep, and I'll have you home in L.A. by day after tomorrow, maybe sooner. And, for chrissake, help me remember to grab two suitcases full of product. Also, there was some miscommunication and a mule was sent out a few days ago about the time we got the assignment. He was due in tonight. We've got to make certain we take all the product and drop it off at an address in Van Horn before we go through the Sierra Blanca checkpoint."

"Should've picked up some things at Abercrombie and Fitch, like I said before," Marty grumbled.

They left the car and began following the road, driver pointing the flashlight straight down. In the clear desert air, Peter Long Grass could see a small glowing circle coming along a ranch road, the jiggle and bounce of the glow indicating someone was on foot and carrying a flashlight.

Winchell Dear had sat in the living room for a long time. His whiskey was gone, and he went back to the kitchen, where he poured a small amount in the glass, looking up at the Regulator clock: 3:45. The long night would soon be over. The fear, the sense of something wrong, must have been all in the imagination of an old man. That sort of thing happened to older people, some inexplicable panic that a certain night might be their last. He'd read that somewhere. Well, he was pretty certain he'd read it somewhere. With the Cadillac gassed and ready to travel, he began thinking about driving up to Las Vegas and playing a little serious poker.

The dog sleeping under the kitchen table had looked up when Winchell walked into the kitchen, putting her head back down after a moment. A night breeze came in through one of the windows facing east, and the dog suddenly jerked her head up again, open-eyed. She got to her feet, walked to the window, sniffed, and growled.

"What's the matter now, girl?"

The dog growled louder, hair on the nape of her neck coming up straight. Winchell Dear slid the .380 Colt from his boot and worked the slide, injecting a cartridge into the chamber, leaving six in the clip. He turned off the kitchen lights and walked to the window, standing above the dog. The dog looked up at him, then out the window, and deepened the intensity of her growl, barking once, then again.

Winchell Dear went into the living room and shut off the last remaining lamps in the house. Looking northwest, he could see lights on in the place where Sonia Dominguez lived. That meant nothing to him, knowing as he did that she always seemed to keep strange hours. He returned to the kitchen, took down his eight-cell portable spotlight from a shelf, and looked out the window where the dog sat, still growling.

Marty had undergone a transformation, the driver noticed. No more complaining, ratcheting himself up to another level, the Marty he'd seen before on other jobs and counted on seeing when the time came for it: tight faced and cool, the shooter ready to do his work. They stumbled along the rough road, shoes filling with dust and slowly tearing apart on rocks and gravel. Anything sharp, and everything on the road seemed to be sharp, poked up and almost through the soles of fine city shoes. So far, they'd missed stepping on mesquite thorns, which would come up and through leather like a nail.

The wind blew, and somewhere on it came the sound of a dog's bark.

"Jesus, what's that?" Marty grabbed the driver's jacket with one hand and stopped him.

"Where, what?"

"Right up ahead, something big and moving."

Instinctively, the driver flashed the light toward where Marty was pointing. "Holy shit!"

A dozen longhorn cattle stood ahead of them and looked back. Some of the steers weighed 1,500 pounds and carried horn spans of six feet.

"Cows, biggest goddamn cows I ever seen, bigger'n a fucking truck!" Marty said. He brought up his Beretta and leveled it toward the cattle.

And maybe for the first time on this trip, in spite of the long drive and the long roads that had brought them through great Texas spaces and should have accustomed him to how marked and different this land was from his usual world, the driver began to get a feeling that he was far out of his element. Inside the Connie, he'd felt control and power and confidence. But now he shivered, and in spite of his size and the Beretta in his hand, he suddenly went small in the forever reach of the high desert, with the wind whipping through stunted trees and the light beam reflecting the eyes of longhorn cattle. Some of the steers were red, some white with black spots, some a combination of all three colors. The longhorns gave no sign of moving or even of fear. They simply stared back at Marty and the driver.

"Well, it doesn't look like they're going to charge or anything," the driver whispered. "We'll cut off around them, go left. That ranch house is only about a hundred yards ahead."

"Yeah, well, notice the lights have gone off."

"You're right. Probably doesn't mean anything. Somebody went to bed, that's all."

For once, things worked out. Marty and the driver detoured around the cattle and found the ranch road again. They were fifty yards from the main house.

Looking out the kitchen window, Winchell Dear had caught the momentary flash of a light out in the desert. His gut jumped, his heartbeat immediately came up thirty points. He saw the light again. It remained steady, directed at something for a few seconds, then disappeared from his view. He moved to one side of the window and watched but could see nothing.

Northwest of the main house, Sonia Dominguez was picking up Pablo Espinosa's breakfast dishes, though he hadn't quite finished eating.

"It's time, old man. *Vamos, ándale.*"

Pablo Espinosa thought of the long day before him and the long road back to Santa Helena and how he would have to tell his story once again to *la migra.* They would be able to prove nothing. He would be home, perhaps by this evening or, with great luck, by late afternoon. Still, it seemed a long risky way to him, as it always did.

Sonia Dominguez cracked the front door and looked toward the main house. It was darkened now; Winchell Dear had finally gone to bed.

"Come," she said to Pablo Espinosa.

He went through the door and onto a road in front of the adobe. Then he turned right and began walking toward the western fence line of the ranch. There he would turn north and follow another ranch road to Route 90. His legs were some rested, but he was still tired. Yet his feet again seemed to have a life of their own, and the sandals began their relentless shuffle, this time toward the border and home.

When she was sure he'd gone, Sonia Dominguez went to her closet and took out a suitcase. She put the case and the old man's pack on her bed. Carefully, she began the process of repackaging and skimming *la mota,* visions before her of a solid brick house in the nicer part of Clear Signal, a place where she could live out her years in comfort and style.

Marty had taken a route around the south side of the main house and worked his way along the wall, past French doors leading into an interior room. The driver moved cautiously around the east side of the building. Inside he could hear a dog barking, and he didn't like that. It might awaken whoever slept within the house. He glanced at the luminous dial of his watch: nearly 4:00.

Marty rounded the house corner and saw lights a quarter mile northwest. The lamps outlined a smaller building, and he knew then where his target was. A figure appeared along the front of the house, and Marty whispered, "See those lights? Down there's where we'll find her."

A voice came back to him: "Who are you, and what do you want?" Not the driver's voice, somebody else's. A man speaking strong and direct.

Forgetting the driver was coming around the other side of the house, Marty fired a three-shot burst — *phoom phoom phoom* — along the wall and stepped backward toward the corner he'd just turned, looking for cover. A flash from near the front door and a .380 slug caught Marty in the upper left shoulder, pistol sound coming an instant later.

"Marty! You all right?" the driver called out, letting Winchell Dear know there was another one out there. All games have their tells.

Not badly hurt, but stumbling backward

from the force of the bullet and surprise, and beginning to fall as he tripped over a honey-suckle vine, Marty could hear the driver's voice somewhere in the night. As he hit the ground, he could also hear another sound, something like the quick, loud rustle of dry leaves as they blow and twist in autumn wind, and one more sound almost obscured by the diamondback's rattle, the hiss of a large snake in full strike position. For Marty, for humans in general, it was as close to hearing the shriek of red hell as is possible.

And then, if lightning could be slowed, if God had given us swifter eyes, it would have looked like this. The diamondback began its strike with mouth closed and fangs folded back. Somewhere in the middle of the javelinlike thrust, the mouth opened to almost 180 degrees, disclosing a flash of white throat and fangs straightening into bite position. The fangs hit Marty in the neck, plunging through the skin just above where the collar of his eighty-dollar white shirt ended. The jaws closed, and the snake, in its own kind of terror and doing what it could to defend itself, injected nearly a full load of venom into a portion of the body constituting virtually the worst possible place a human can be bitten, directly into a carotid artery feeding oxygenated blood to the brain. Marty screamed and tried to stand. He got to his hands and knees, still clutching the Beretta in his right hand, pulling the trigger involuntarily and scattering shots into the dirt, hitting nothing. The diamondback, wild with its own fear, struck again, this time stabbing into Marty's cheek and releasing the remainder of its venom load, after which it began a quick backward crawl into the night and away from what had threatened it.

On his feet then and screaming again, Marty did exactly the wrong thing, though not much could have helped him at that point except medical attention, and probably not even that given the bite locations. He began to run in no particular direction, just running crazy into the night and firing the Beretta in random directions, trying to escape the realization of all his fears coming true. He was suffering pain in the bite areas and a heartbeat rising up and over two hundred, partly from the venom and partly from terror. Simultaneously, his blood pressure began to fall, and the touch of his own hand told him he was already swelling on the neck and face.

Marty had forgotten entirely about his bullet wound, from which no pain seemed to be emanating but from which some bleeding was occurring. He ran farther, stumbling toward the smaller house, thinking some kind of help had to be found. He ran and stumbled and came to a staggering halt when the point of a spear fashioned from a long straight branch of mesquite plunged through his chest and into his heart. Peter Long Grass let go of the shaft as Marty fell.

The driver, having no idea what had happened, stayed as calm as he could and tried to refocus himself. The one thing he always had been told was this: You're the cleaner; we count on you to get the job done, to finish whatever task we send you to do. And the driver was good at that, at finishing. He had been in tough scrapes before. After the shots and Marty's first scream, he began jogging toward the small building northwest of the main house. Whatever had occurred, Marty would have to take care of himself for now.

More lights were coming on inside the adobe. He could see the profile of someone looking out a window. Get closer, be certain, *finish.* He smashed his 230 pounds through the door, saw a woman, and knew instantly she was the target. She stood there in her nightdress, pressing herself against the kitchen sink fifteen feet away, eyes wide.

Breathing hard, the driver flicked his Beretta to automatic and began to swing it up to firing position, preparing to kill a woman who thirty-eight years earlier had given him life. Near where Sonia Dominguez stood, a rear door banged open, and a tall old man in a white shirt and blue suspenders leaned around the sill, firing two rounds from some kind of pistol, then ducking back outside. Neither bullet hit the driver . . . but the arrow did, slamming into the middle of his back and causing him to lunge forward a step with its impact. He turned to see a dark shape running through the night and fired a quick three-round burst, all the while wondering what was causing the strange sensation in his back.

Now, and once more, the sound of Winchell Dear's pistol as he leaned through the kitchen door — this time from behind the driver, who was facing outside — and this time both bullets hit, one near the arrow wound, the second higher and toward his right shoulder.

Confused and reacting to the most immediate threat, the driver managed to turn back toward the pistol, vaguely noticing that the woman had disappeared and seeing only the open rear door swinging on its hinges in the night wind. Wheeling around once more to the darkness outside, he caught the four-inch blade of a well-sharpened skinning knife in his throat, driven hard and home by the strong right arm of Peter Long Grass. Simultaneously, the Beretta was ripped from his hand and thrown into the darkness. A knee hit his groin, and the driver went down, dying fast there in the doorway of a high-desert adobe.

Peter Long Grass gave a quiet grunt of distaste, of hate, for everything the world had become and kicked his heavy boot full into the driver's face.

FOURTEEN

In the main house of the Two Pair Ranch, Winchell Dear carefully packs a suitcase, his good suits and shirts and ties, and removes twenty thousand dollars from a floor safe in his bedroom closet. The Cadillac is oiled and gassed and will be pointed toward Las Vegas the following dawn. Six miles farther south on the ranch, Peter Long Grass lies on his sleeping bag, hands behind his head, the day's images replaying in his mind.

Neither of them much caring for complications in their lives, he and the old man dumped a Lincoln Continental emptied of gas and oil, but containing two bodies and two Berettas, down a mine shaft five miles from the main house. On top of that potpourri were tossed brown suitcases and a knapsack. Using the front-end loader on the ranch tractor, they covered all the shoddy with ten feet of dirt and rocks.

As for Sonia Dominguez, who knows, who

cares? She disappeared into the darkness that early morning. A bank account in Clear Signal was closed five hours later, and a bus ticket to Presidio, Texas, was purchased. Since Ojinaga lies just over the border, perhaps she was heading for Mexico and a fine brick house in a coastal town.

The last item packed in Winchell Dear's suitcase is a copy of his will. In Vegas he intends to have it rewritten, leaving most of the ranch to Lucinda Miller, as before, but also two thousand acres and an access easement to a man named Peter Long Grass, whose address will be shown as "Southernmost Canyon (Diablo Canyon); Two Pair Ranch; Clear Signal, Texas."

When he told the Indian of his intentions, Peter Long Grass nodded and said, "I will care for the land and bring venison to your willow tree."

While Winchell Dear packs his bag, while an Indian lies in contemplation in a rugged canyon, a man named Pablo Espinosa rides comfortably in the rear seat of a border patrol Jeep Cherokee and looks out the window at a three-quarter moon on its way to full and yellow flowers beginning to open in the late dusk. He has decided this was his last run to *el Norte.* Never allow greed to influence your decisions, his uncle used to tell him, and Pablo Espinosa judged he had saved enough for his dream of a small hacienda in the cool wet mountains of the Sierra Madre, a place to show his grandchildren, who would hold his hand and walk with him in the forest and fish clear streams.

So in mountains that rose volcanically centuries past and ever oblivious to the ways of humans, the night plays itself like an old Victrola song, a high-desert song: easy wind through the mesquite and scrub cedar, a coyote's howl answered or joined seconds later by other coyotes, and the almost imperceptible scrape of loose gravel where a seven-foot diamondback rattlesnake named Luther crosses a ranch road and winds through a stand of evening primrose.

ACKNOWLEDGMENTS

Thanks to my agent, David Vigliano, for his suggestions about improving the manuscript. And I feel a faraway, nostalgic sense of gratitude to the remote high-desert ranch where I once made my home, a place that provided me with the ideas and language for this book.

ABOUT THE AUTHOR

Robert James Waller lives in the Texas Hill Country and pursues his interests in economics, mathematics, photography, and music, as the spirit moves him. In the evenings, he wades Hill Country streams with his fly rod.